For Maritsa,
With love

Enid Richemont

For Maritsa, With Love

SIMON &
SCHUSTER

Simon & Schuster, London

First published in Great Britain by Simon & Schuster UK Ltd, 2001
A Viacom Company

Text copyright © 2000 by Enid Richemont
Cover illustration copyright © 2001 Ian Winstanley

1 3 5 7 9 10 8 6 4 2

Simon and Schuster UK Ltd
Africa House
64-78 Kingsway
London WC2B 6AH

Simon & Schuster
Australia Sydney

A CIP catalogue record for this book is available from the British Library

ISBN 0 689 836368

Printed by WS Bookwell Ltd, Finland

For Jude, Alan, Jeremy, Lynn, Alfie and Anna.
For David, my irreplaceable technical support
and Sophie at Ed Victor -

and for Maritsa
wherever she may be,

with love.

CHAPTER ONE

The posh suburbs of Paris were a dead loss.

By the time the trains had reached La Defense, the inner-city mob with its rich tourist pickings would have fizzled out, and they'd be left with nothing but well-off suburban wives and sharp-faced young women in stylish clothes. Not many soft hearts to be melted there; not much to be wheedled out of those designer bags or those soft leather satchels.

But the three of them couldn't work all the time, and often, like today, they stayed on just for the ride — all the way to St Germain and all the way back. They enjoyed spying on the balconies which at one point were level with the train, and speeding across the two wide loops of the river. The ride was always free because they never got out, and even if an inspector turfed them off, there were plenty of other trains.

The girl kicked off her ill-fitting shoes and curled her bare toes around the edge of the seat. Her pale, pointed face with its dark, thickly browed eyes, was further narrowed by two skinny, red-ribbonned braids in front of gold-ringed ears that held back a tangle of long, almost black hair. Pretending to be alone, she hugged her knees and rocked gently with the rhythm of the train, her brightly flowered skirts billowing round her like a tent.

. At the other end of the carriage, the two boys were larking about noisily, offering nothing, not even displaying the note, Nikolas not even bothering to play the mouth organ. Maritsa sighed. Kids, she thought: just stupid kids. She wasn't really with them; they really had nothing to do with her. She could see the other passengers pointedly ignoring them, scanning their newspapers with fake concentration or staring fixedly out of windows.

But one woman looked up and, in a fine display of charity, smiled at them indulgently. It was a big mistake. In an instant they were on her, grubby fingers pawing at her fur coat.

'Nice mother, give us a couple of francs.'

Maritsa shook her head. They would never do it properly. They were loud and aggressive and they scared people. When she worked a carriage, she was pleading and gentle, remembering her manners, saying 'please' and 'thank you' and 'God bless you' in her very best French, for Maritsa knew that soft words could often prise open even the tightest purse. People sometimes gave the boys money in order to be rid of them, but it was she, Maritsa, who made the real loot. Soon she'd be grown-up. Then she'd work alone and keep the money for herself, and spend it on all the things she wanted...

The woman, meanwhile, had stiffened. She did not like to be called 'mother'; the word spoilt her carefully constructed image – the smooth mask of her face and the creamy fingers immaculately tipped with scarlet. Moreover, the kids' breath smelt of cheap sweets, and if they could afford to buy sweets, why were they begging? Like those so-called homeless, she thought, who wore placards round their necks. Able-bodied young people, just too lazy to work.

Oh, she'd been wrong to smile at these two, she could see that now. She drew herself further back against the seat. 'Go away,' she said firmly.

Nikolas grinned, revealing lumpy pink gum-gaps and a small flash of gold. He draped an arm around Stefan's shoulder, like that gangster he'd once seen on TV. They'd have fun with this one.

'Ten francs would do,' he pleaded, holding the mouth organ like a gun.

They were only kids, the woman told herself nervously.

'Or twenty... How about a twenty?'

'Give us a twenty, mother.' Stefan ran a sticky finger across the smooth leather of the woman's bag. 'You got plenty in there.'

The train surfaced into sunshine and Maritsa found her lashes suddenly beaded with points of light, so that for a moment everything she looked at was framed with little pearls. The light shimmered and danced over a bunch of plastic cherries pinned to the jacket of the girl sitting next to her. They looked sticky, juicy, almost edible, irresistible. Maritsa put out a finger to touch them.

Immediately the girl shifted, drawing herself in. Didn't these gypsy brats have fleas?

From the other end of the carriage came the woman's voice, loud and with an edge of panic: 'If you do not go away this instant, I'll pull the alarm.' She was attracting attention. Heads were beginning to turn.

Nikolas immediately backed down.

'Only a couple of francs, mother,' he wheedled.

'Lousy beggars,' someone grumbled.

'Guard'll fix them and out they'll go, the whole bunch of them, girl as well...'

Maritsa had had enough. As the train slowed to enter Nanterre, she swung her bag over her shoulder and marched up to the boys.

'We get out here,' she said pointedly, speaking in Rom.

They turned. They gawped.

'Bossy, aren't you?' sneered Stefan.

'You can't order us around,' said Nikolas. 'You should treat us with respect,' added Stefan. 'Our mama feeds you, remember.'

The train slid along the platform and stopped.

'Well, *I'm* getting out,' said Maritsa with dignity. 'You two can do whatever you like.'

The sight of her discarded shoes gave Stefan an idea. He suddenly ran forward, grabbed them and hurled them across the carriage. When the automatic doors opened, he bowed. 'Get out then, your majesty,' he taunted. 'Got no shoes now, have you?'

Maritsa hesitated. By the time she'd scrabbled around for her shoes, those doors would have closed.

In a sudden rage, she forced herself, barefoot, through the narrowing gap. This would teach them, she thought; this would scare them. She grinned. If those two kids turned up without her at the end of the day, they'd be walloped. She might not be their blood sister but she still lived with their family. And they were part of a *kumpania*. They shared the same base, they ate together, they worked together and they were supposed to look after each other.

Her feet met the icy concrete of the platform. She tugged at the folds of her skirts, still trapped between the doors, and the fabric tore as it came away. The train began to move, gathering speed. Maritsa stood and watched the two grinning masks at the window blurring, then vanishing. The empty rails glittered like swords. Suddenly she felt exhilarated. She was alone. At last she was alone.

She turned and looked, and saw a day that was silver and blue. The air was like crystal, the December light dancing and sparkling on every surface. Unable to keep still, Maritsa began skipping along the platform, excitement zizzling inside her like the champagne bubbles she'd seen in the ads.

She worked it out. The boys would soon be back. They'd cross over at the next station, take the inner-city train and come back to pick her up; after all, Maritsa had the bag with the morning's pickings. Not much, but enough. And naturally they'd expect her to be waiting, for how far could she get without shoes? It had only been a joke, they'd tell her. They would bring her shoes back (lucky for them, thought Maritsa, that those shoes hadn't hit anyone, or things might have gone badly). They'd wave them in front of her, laughing, teasing.

Well, too bad, Maritsa thought. Because she wouldn't be there.

She glanced up at the indicator and worked out the patterns of letters and numbers. The next train to St Germain was already announced. Good, she thought, so the game could begin. Hide-and-seek, she supposed it might be called. Maritsa never played – playing was for kids and she was nearly thirteen – but this was a serious game, to teach those kids a lesson. She'd keep to their usual route, and she'd work as well, so no money would be lost and no one could complain.

And she'd play fair: she would leave them plenty of clues. Whenever she changed trains, she would draw them a *patrin* – a direction sign – with the pencil stub she had in the bag. The boys knew all the *patrins* by heart. If they were too dumb to spot them, too bad. She was sick of their teasing and their constant squabbling. She was sick of hearing about their family's generosity and her mother's shame.

The next few hours, she decided, until they caught up, belonged to her. Maritsa.

Inside the glass-fronted waiting room, a couple of women noticed the small gypsy girl in her thin top of purple velvet and her long, flowered skirts.

'Look. That child has bare feet. In this weather,' said one.

The second woman was unmoved. 'They'll do anything for publicity.'

But the first woman had just dropped off her own daughter, warmly dressed and snugly booted, at the house of a friend, so she took two ten-franc coins out of her purse, walked across to Maritsa and slipped them into her hand.

Maritsa stared down at the coins. She couldn't believe her luck. She had asked for nothing. She hadn't even shown her note; it was still crumpled up inside her pocket.

The woman was looking at her feet and shaking her head.

Suddenly Maritsa caught on. Bare feet, what a prop!

Today, she thought, she would do *really* well.

The indicator on the other side of the platform lit up and she closed her eyes, crossed her fingers and prayed. If those kids came back now, her whole scheme would be spoilt. As if in reply, a train arrived on her own line. Even the saints approved, she thought happily, and she remembered to thank them politely as she climbed on board.

When the doors closed, she pulled down one of the little hinged seats and sat astride it, her bare legs dangling from beneath her skirts like the limbs of a rag doll. The first down train to Paris passed on the adjacent line and she thanked the saints again, because she knew the boys would be on it, and that she had a head start. And at the next station, she coolly walked across the platform and got on the city train which was standing there, waiting just for her.

It was due to leave in three minutes. One or two people, already irritated by the delay, stood at the doors and glared impotently at the indicator. Maritsa assessed the possibilities – suburban housewives going into town to do their Christmas shopping and lots of schoolkids because it was Wednesday. Fat purses, but the kids would be too much of a distraction. No point, she decided, in working that lot. As usual, there would be better pickings after they'd passed La Defense.

The doors closed and the train moved slowly out of the station. Maritsa drew up her knees and tucked her toes under her skirts for warmth. Then she looked at the girl on the opposite seat, a girl of about her own age, with a woman in a fur-collared coat who was probably her mama.

What was it like, Maritsa wondered, to have a real family? Her own mother was just a fantasy, coloured occasionally by the things other people said. She'd been pretty. Beautiful. *Sexy.* Well, she must have been sexy if they said all those things about her. A disgrace to the tribe, they said. A wanton. Unclean. A judgement on her that she'd died young... And the Blessed Virgin might know who Maritsa's father was but no one else did. Some *gadjo* boy, the rumour went, and what could be worse than that?

Maybe it had been God, joked Maritsa to herself. After all, it wouldn't be the first time...

She began studying the girl, her glossy black puffa jacket and her olive-green stretch pants, her hair layered and streaked, small silver studs in her ears and her fingers glowing in scarlet wool. Where did she live? wondered Maritsa. In a gingerbread house with pierced wooden shutters and a little square garden? Perhaps an apartment with one of those balconies they liked to spy on. What was it like to live that way, to stay in one place all the time, to go to a school? What was it like to be one of *them,* the *gadjé*? She searched the girl's face for some kind of an answer.

'That gypsy's staring at me,' complained the girl.

Maritsa stuck out her tongue.

'Let's go and sit somewhere else,' said the woman. 'Come, *chérie...*'

Just before Nanterre-Précture, the train dived underground. From now on, and until it had crossed the city, it would become the Métro. Maritsa relaxed. Soon the smug, suburban faces would be outnumbered, and by the time they got to Etoile there would be tourists again. In the city there were always tourists: sometimes more and sometimes less, but always enough. In preparation, she brought out her note, carefully smoothing the crumpled paper.

The note was a sad one. Heartbreaking:

I AM 11 YEARS OLD (her breasts didn't show yet and she was still small. Anyway, if you were older, nobody cared.) MY FATHER IS DED. MY MOTHER IS ILL. I HAVE FIVE BRUTHERS AND SISTERS AND WE HAVE NO MONEY FOR FOOD.

The note was freshly written each day, the message varying with the imagination of the writer. Sometimes Maritsa would write it herself, carefully copying the loops and squiggles from some previous note. She enjoyed writing; she wanted to learn to do it properly, even though the mama didn't think it really mattered. She wanted to learn reading as well. She knew most of the letters already. One day, she thought, she would make lots of money and keep it in some secret place. Then she could read, write, do whatever she liked...

The doors opened and closed, opened and closed. Each time she looked over the fresh supply of passengers. Not a bad lot now, it was worth a try. She stood up, modestly lifting her skirts slightly to show off her bare feet. How good it felt to be working without the boys.

And, like an actress, she pulled on what she knew was a sad kid's face and slowly, wanly, walked through the carriage displaying her note. Most people ignored it, but one or two tourists softened and smiled (wasn't it nearly Christmas?) and dropped a few coins into her outstretched hand.

And by the time the train came rolling into the grand marble station of Etoile, Maritsa had collected quite a fistful.

CHAPTER TWO

Maritsa got out.

She paused for a moment to count her takings while the crowd jostled past her. Someone trod on her foot and she yelped and cursed them. Then she dropped the money into the bag. Thirty-five francs. Not bad. Not bad at all.

She moved on. The long passageways could be even more profitable than the trains. There she dawdled, running her fingers along the cold, slippery tiles, savouring the pleasure of being alone, allowing herself to be hypnotized by the patterns on the wall. If the boys had been there they would have nagged: 'Come on, Maritsa, come *on...*' Now she could take all the time in the world.

But eventually the day's pickings would have to be made. She chose a pitch close to an old man in a greasy black suit who was coaxing a melancholy tune out of an ancient fiddle. Maritsa listened curiously. His music made her think of the stray animals no one wanted that sometimes came wandering on to the travellers' site. And it made her think of sad, half-remembered things, of always being moved on, of never really belonging, and of all those poor homeless *gadjé* with the hopeless eyes who were so rotten at begging.

For Maritsa had always known how to do it properly, how to take advantage of an old man's sad, off-key music, how to touch people's hearts. She arranged herself now on the ground, spreading her skirts, taking care to show off her naked, dirty feet, and her dark eyes became those of a lost puppy, large and pleading. It was impossible to look into those eyes without feeling a bit guilty, without offering a coin or two, and she knew it. Soon the little pile grew.

The old man stopped playing and scowled. 'This is *my* pitch!' he spat. 'I was here first.'

Maritsa scooped up the takings and tucked them away in her *posoti*, the secret pouch hidden inside one of her skirts. It was fair, she'd made enough, and she *had* been spoiling his act. They might have worked together, she thought, but he wasn't the type.

As she walked away she could already hear him muttering, 'Filthy gypsy! Gypsy thief!'

Maritsa didn't care. That little pantomime must have earned her at least fifty francs. Seventy, maybe. Almost as much as she would have made in a day with the boys. They might yell and curse when they finally caught up with her, but they couldn't say she'd wasted her time.

She began to work it out. Some of the loot she would keep

for herself. How much? How much would be fair? Half? Why not? After all, she'd earned it – bare feet were no joke. Perhaps she should keep it all... No. If she turned up empty-handed, the boys would still know. And, later, the mama might hold her down and search; she had done it before.

She could keep it all, she supposed, and never go back. She could hide it in some secret place. She could even put it in a bank. The thought made her grin. Banks were for the *gadjé*. If you gave banks gypsy money, they'd only steal it. Better stay with the *kumpania*, she thought. Better stay with your own kind.

So what was the next move? Trocadéro, she decided, taking a risk. It was one of their favourite runs. There were always tourists at the Troc and the boys would be sure to go there, even if they'd missed her *patrin* at Etoile. She was playing very fair, Maritsa thought virtuously. She hadn't once cheated.

On the multiple escalators in the grand central hall, people were drifting up and down like sleepwalkers, like dreamers. Maritsa sat on a step and drifted with them, scratching the soles of her feet against the thin metal slats. To change lines, she fished out a grubby ticket which she fed to the machine. A crocodile of little kids followed her through – an *école maternelle* on its Wednesday afternoon outing. By the time they'd caught up with her, they were already out of step and fooling around. Maritsa drew in her toes and flattened herself against the wall.

Bare feet were all very well as props, but they were beginning to be a problem.

She exercised the same caution on the crowded platform, but on the train she relaxed, squatting on one of the pull-out seats and tucking her toes away safely.

At Trocadéro the station stalls were gaudy with souvenirs. Eiffel towers in silver and gold lay heaped up in trays. They twinkled and swung from chains. They dangled from a hundred keyrings lettered PARIS or lay trapped inside round plastic bubbles which made snowstorms when you shook them.

Maritsa went into the newspaper kiosk and bought two bars of chocolate – she was beginning to feel hungry. After she'd worked the Troc, she decided, she would eat properly. A couple of sandwiches. Perhaps a pancake with butter and jam. After all, she had the cash.

And maybe by then the boys would have caught up with her...

After she'd finished the chocolate, she wiped her mouth carefully with the back of her hand. Unlike them, she would never eat while she was working. How could you expect people to take you seriously if you stood there chewing like a goat? She took up a good position, squatting on the floor with her two grimy feet pushed well forward for effect.

A kindly woman, towing two small children, threw her a

couple of coins.

The children stared. 'Why has that girl got no shoes?' asked one, pointing.

The woman smiled apologetically at Maritsa and hurried them away.

A group of Swedish backpackers glanced down at her curiously. She handed them the note but they shook their heads and acted stupid. One of them threw her a fifty-centime piece. Maritsa looked at it scornfully, then spat; a waste of time to pick that thing up.

Irritated, she decided to try her luck outside. It was cheating, she knew; the boys would never think of looking for her up there. They never worked outside, not even in summer. Up there was the women's territory – each day they would share babies, wrap them up warmly, put a drop of brandy in their feed to keep them contented, and sit for hours on the pavement outside the rich department stores. The Métro was for kids; everyone knew that.

Guiltily, Maritsa scribbled a slick *patrin* over the tiled wall. The message was quite clear; the boys had only to use their eyes. Then she climbed the steps and walked out into the street.

For the first few moments she just stood there, blinking into the sunshine. It was as if someone had switched on all the lights, illuminating everything so brightly that it almost hurt her eyes. The pavements were dazzling white and rimed with frost, the sky was china blue, and the big statues outside the Palais de Chaillot glittered gold in the sun. In a trance, Maritsa walked up the broad white steps, past the golden statues and over to the balustrade.

There, just below where she stood, fountains drew high shimmering arcs across formal lawns and shrubs. Beyond the gardens there was a road; along it, Maritsa could see traffic moving restlessly, constantly. Beyond that, trees marked the edge of the river, and a bridge spanned it, and then came another park, more green shapes, more trees, but straddling it all, with its splayed metal feet, stood the tower, the great tower, like some dumb giant, with his pinpoint head thrust into the sky.

Maritsa had seen it many times, but never like that – so sparkling new, so huge, so far away and yet so close that she felt if she put out her hands she could touch it. Spray from the fountains blew into her face. She caught it on her tongue; it tasted icy and metallic. Suddenly she wanted to fly through that iridescent spray, to fly across the road and the river and the parks, to soar upwards and land on the giant's head. She spread out her hands, making wings, reaching for the water rainbows. One day, when she was rich, she thought, she might fly in an aeroplane...

She shook herself. All that was kids' stuff. And she'd never get rich without working.

She turned and ran an expert eye over the scene. She saw the photographers performing their strange ballet of crouches and contortions and little backward steps. She saw the African traders patiently spreading out identical woodcarvings on identical rugs. She saw country families out sightseeing; lovers kissing on the steps; a gaggle of kids on rollerblades.

A flock of American tourists was herded across the terrace to view the tower – middle-aged ladies with soft hearts and fat purses. Maritsa moved in close, posing deliberately in front of them, showing off her bare feet. She unfolded the scribbled note and showed it. Her eyes became sorrowful and she blinked, as if holding back tears.

The women passed the note around.

'Is anyone's French good enough for this, girls?' one of them called out.

'My – father – is – dead,' someone translated haltingly.

'Will you look at this kid's feet?' exclaimed the lady with lavender hair. 'Let's have a round, girls,' and she put out her hand. Purses and handbags instantly snapped open. 'Think of your grandchildren back home,' urged the lavender-haired lady. 'Would you like them to go around with no shoes? And in the middle of winter?'

When they had all given, the lavender-haired lady took a

fifty-franc note from her wallet, made a parcel of the money and handed it to Maritsa.

'Go buy yourself some shoes, honey,' she said. 'Or at least some hot food.'

Stunned by her good fortune, Maritsa stared at the money in her hand.

'Thank you,' she whispered. Then she remembered her lines. 'God bless you,' she said. 'And the saints bless you and the Holy Virgin bless you. And a happy Christmas!'

The 'happy Christmas', at least, they understood. Pleased with themselves, they smiled and called out, 'Happy Christmas to you! *Bon Noël*, honey,' as they walked away.

Maritsa held the money tightly in her fist. How much was there? She didn't dare imagine.

A street photographer, jealous of her success, glowered at her. 'Piss off, gypsy!'

Fearful suddenly for her newly acquired wealth, Maritsa began to run. She pattered down the steps of the Métro. She scuttled like a rat into its comforting darkness. She didn't feel safe until she'd pushed her ticket through the machine and crossed the barrier. Only then, on her own territory and behind the protective screen of her skirts, did she examine her takings: eighty-seven francs fifty. Eighty-seven francs, and she had made it all in five minutes. Eighty-seven francs. She was *loaded!*

She stowed it away in her bag. All that money, all that loot. She gave a little skip out of pure joy. She was good. She'd always known she was good. She skipped and skipped. Wait till she showed the boys, she thought; they'd be speechless, for once. Then there would be the usual squabbles about how much to spend on sweets and chewing gum and how much to hand over. And there were things Maritsa wanted for herself: silk flowers and sequins to sew on her velvet top, African earrings with little bells from one of the traders, glossy magazines full of pictures, eyeshadow, even lipstick...

Still daydreaming, she blindly followed people on to a train. Only when she sat down did she spell out its destination: N-A-T-I-O-N. Nation.

She really *had* meant to keep to their usual routine...

Maritsa shrugged. Today was special. Today she was breaking all the rules. She would be a good girl, yes, but later. Not now. After all, she argued, she'd left them enough clues.

Stations passed. Maritsa amused herself by trying to match their names with the letters on the map: Dupleix, Cambronne, Pasteur... Words, words – Paris was full of them. She often wondered how it felt to get your stories that way. For the other people, the *gadjé*, never seemed to *tell* tales; perhaps they forgot them so quickly that they had to write them down. The *gadjé* stuffed their heads with printed words, the mama said, and too many words were bad for people. Like eating too much. Like boozing. Like too many boyfriends.

At Denfert-Rochereau, Maritsa blinked as the train emerged briefly from the tunnels. Golden sunlight filtered through naked trees and picked out garlands of stone roses on the curly iron balconies.

She changed trains. She knew where she was going now — she was going to Luxembourg. There was a big park at Luxembourg. And where there was a park, there would be a pancake stall. Today she would feast on pancakes: not just ordinary ones with melted butter and crunchy sugar, but those special ones with chocolate and strawberry jam and purée of chestnuts. She would gobble up her share of the money; the boys couldn't take that away. She would stuff herself on pancakes, gorge until she couldn't cram in another grain of sugar, another lick of chestnut.

And after that, she decided, she'd be good.

CHAPTER THREE

The train for Luxembourg was one of the old ones and its dirty yellow carriages clattered and swayed. Maritsa sat staring at the grey lines of cable snaking along the black tunnel walls.

At the station she ran up a short flight of steps and out into the street, and to her delight, found already in front of her the wrought-iron railings that marked the edges of the Luxembourg Gardens. Outside the main gates stood a man with a bouquet of silver balloons. Children jostled around him, eyes fixed on the fat shining spheres bobbing above their heads.

Maritsa hesitated, tempted. She could afford one. *If* she really wanted one, she could have one. But she didn't really want one, of course she didn't. How silly she'd look — a girl of nearly thirteen with a kid's balloon!

She turned her back on them quickly and walked through the gates, and the sounds of the street and the noise of the traffic melted like magic. On her right, through a tracery of leafless trees, stood the Luxembourg Palace, its walls honeyed by the winter sun. Little curly-backed chairs, robbed of their usual occupants by the cold, huddled together in sad twos and threes, and under the shelter of a stone goddess, a couple of old men shared a bottle of cheap wine.

Maritsa slowed down. The gravel was clinging to the soles of her feet and lodging painfully between her toes. But the path she was on opened out into a terrace, with a green-painted wooden stall. She could already smell the pancakes.

Forgetting about her feet, she ran up to it.

'One jam pancake and one chocolate pancake,' she demanded breathlessly.

The man behind the counter shook his head.

'One at a time, one at a time, young lady,' he grumbled. 'Can't make them any faster.'

She watched him pour the batter on the griddle, spreading it out thinly with a flat knife. When the pancake was ready, he put a spoonful of jam in the middle, folded it into a triangle, wrapped it in a twist of paper and handed it to her. Then he poured out the batter for the next one.

'Chocolate?'

Maritsa nodded, her mouth already full.

The man suddenly had second thoughts. 'You got the money, gypsy kid?'

''Course,' mumbled Maritsa. 'Got plenty.'

He ladled out the chocolate and folded the second pancake. A sparrow landed on the counter and he threw it a crust of bread. Jerking its head from side to side, it pecked out a large piece of crumb, but half-way back to the trees dropped it.

'Too ambitious, that fellow,' said the man, and Maritsa nodded wisely, enjoying the sound of the long word and wondering what it meant. She bit into the second pancake. Chocolate oozed out and curled a brown moustache over her upper lip.

'Twenty francs,' said the man, suddenly brisk and business-like.

'I want a chestnut one,' said Maritsa. 'I want an Orangina too.'

The man looked at her suspiciously.

'You sure you've got enough money for all that?'

She showed him.

He scooped it up instantly. Then, shaking his head, he poured out the batter once again.

'You're a lucky girl,' he said. 'I'm packing up at four. Going home. Too cold for me.' He folded the pancake and slammed down the can of Orangina. 'It's true, isn't it? what they say about you lot,' he muttered. 'Well-off. Rich. Rolling in it! Begged or nicked it all from decent folk – even you kids...'

Maritsa shrugged. Begging was a job, like any other. They were all the same, the *gadjé*. 'You make pancakes; I beg,' she could have told him, but she didn't bother. It was just a waste of time.

She slurped up the last dregs of the Orangina and threw the can into the bin. The man was already packing up, folding down the counter, locking the wooden shutters. The sun was red-gold now. Soon it would be dark. Soon the park would be closed.

Maritsa moved away, wanting to explore, wanting to see more before they locked up the gates. A girl in a long coat came mincing out of the shadows, walking a Siamese cat on a thin silver lead. Maritsa made a cat's sex noises and the animal froze, staring at her in terror. Maritsa grinned. She wasn't working now, she didn't have to play the sad kid, she didn't have to be well behaved.

Three middle-aged men in track suits came panting down the path and she ran alongside them, teasing them with exaggerated heavy breathing. 'Pouff-pouff!' she went, laughing at their pink, sweaty faces and their floppy bellies emblazonned with sporting slogans. 'Pouff-pouff!' she gasped loudly. 'Pouff-pouff!'

A line of stone statues stood silhouetted against the sunset. Intrigued, Maritsa left the joggers in peace and ran up to it. She found herself standing at the top of a broad flight of stairs, looking down at a lake. The lake was a mirror for the brilliant sky, but all round it stood the melancholy groups of curly-backed chairs, empty, waiting for spring.

Half-way up the steps, a couple of fashion photographers had set up their equipment. An auburn-haired girl in a violet bodysuit and high heels sat astride one of the chairs, watching them.

'Can we speed things up?' she called out. 'It's freezing!'

One of the men ran down to her.

'Try this, *chérie*.' He struck an exaggerated pose.

The girl imitated, changed, posed, strutted, thrust out hips, breasts, stuck out her tongue and waggled her kid-gloved fingers.

The photographers opened a black leather case and brought out a scarlet cape.

'Jump!' yelled the man with the camera, and the girl jumped.

The scarlet cape flew. The auburn hair danced. The camera click-clicked.

Why, *anyone* could do that, thought Maritsa scornfully. I could do it. I could do it a lot better than her.

The girl stopped jumping and collapsed on to the chair. The two men had a brief discussion, drawing mysterious shapes in the air.

'OK. Let's try this one. Take your shoes off.'

The girl sighed and removed them, throwing them on to the steps. 'Don't ask me to jump into the lake,' she said. 'Because I'm not going to!'

They grinned.

'Not quite that. Just stand on the edge. That's right. Now dip your toe into the water.'

The girl grimaced. Then she spread her arms sideways, balancing on one leg, and dipped in her toe. 'Ouch!' she squealed. 'Ice!'

She shook her bare foot, sprayed silver against orange. The cameras click-clicked.

The shoes lay where they'd fallen. They were made of violet suede. The heels were long and tapering, and across the toes there was a curved inset of silver-dyed leather. They were the most beautiful shoes Maritsa had ever seen and she couldn't take her eyes off them.

She edged down the steps. She needed shoes. She needed shoes badly. She needed them more than that girl down there.

The men were too absorbed in their work to notice.

'Move a little this way. Look up. Laugh. Great!'

Maritsa reached the step where the shoes were lying. The girl suddenly spotted her.

'There's a kid, a gypsy kid.'

The men turned round.

Instantly Maritsa spread out her skirts and sat down over the shoes like a broody hen. Then she put on a pleading face. 'Can I watch?' she asked. 'Please?'

The men shrugged.

'If you behave yourself,' said one.

'Keep an eye on the equipment, then,' said his friend

cynically. 'Pinch anything, that lot.'

Maritsa pushed her hands inside her skirts and felt around for the shoes. She ran her fingers along them, trying to guess at their size; if they didn't fit, it would be tragic. But they felt right. They had to be right. They were too beautiful not to be.

The men walked down to talk to the girl. One of them turned and gave Maritsa a sharp look. 'Don't touch a thing!'

Maritsa shook her head vigorously. 'I wouldn't,' she said.

Carefully she eased up one shoe and tucked its toe behind the waistband of her skirt, puffing out her stomach to hold it tightly. The other one followed.

'That's the lot for today,' said one of the men. 'Too dark to do any more on these,' and he started folding up the tripod.

Maritsa stood shakily, clutching her middle. She began walking up the steps.

'Where did you put my shoes?' asked the girl, and Maritsa fled.

She darted into the twilight trees. Her heart was pounding. She was a thief now. What would they do if they caught her? Take her to the police. And what was prison like? Gypsies would be beaten up in prison, she was sure of that. They always were where she'd come from, so why should France be any different?. And how long would they keep her there? A year? Ten years?

She was back on one of the paths now, crashing into an

embracing couple. The shoes dropped and she nearly tripped over them; she picked them up with trembling fingers and stuffed them into her bag. Behind her she could hear voices. How much time did she have? She ran faster. The little stones were like sharp pins and her feet were cold and sore but she didn't stop running. Through the gates. Up the street. Down the steps and into the Métro.

Along the tiled passageway she found herself a secret corner. She turned to the wall, carefully took out the shoes and put them on. They fitted: of course they did. She tried walking, mincing, arching her feet to accommodate the very high heels. Her skirts swayed and her feet flashed silver and violet. Maritsa watched her feet with delight. No one in the world had such beautiful shoes. All the other girls would want them. Somehow she would have to keep them hidden, but how could she hide anything from the boys?

The boys...

She wondered vaguely where they were now, and if they'd found her *patrins*, for it was already evening...

Two girls strolled past, arm in arm, one of them talking and giggling into a mobile phone. They wore glittery tights and their hair was caught back with little feathered clips, but they didn't have shoes as beautiful as Maritsa's. Maritsa followed them, pretending she was with them. She might put her hair up with fancy clips like that, change her skirts for a mini like the immodest *gadjé* girls, buy herself one of those coloured fake-fur jackets – then no one would dare call her a dirty gypsy. But would it change her inside? She sighed. There were so many ways of being and she wanted to try them all. Even living in a house; she could always move on. After all, she might only be half-gypsy. Her father (as people so often reminded her) could have been anyone. An English milord. An American cowboy. A French pop star...

Lost in her thoughts, Maritsa followed the girls along the subway, up the steps and out on to the opposite side of the street. Across the road, the *gardien* was seeing the last people out of the park, ceremoniously locking the big iron gates. The night was icy, the streetlamps were frosted diamonds, but the windows of shops and cafés were orange fires, warm and inviting. And there was an air of jollity about the crowds, who seemed to move a little closer for warmth and talk a little more loudly because it would soon be Christmas and they could almost hear the angels singing and the bells ringing through the clear winter air.

The two girls melted into the crowd, but Maritsa didn't care, for she was part of the street crowd, too, with her beautiful new shoes. She could be going out for the evening. She could be meeting her boyfriend, the boyfriend *she* had chosen, not the mama, not the tribe. They would walk slowly, arms entwined, gazing at each other like those lovers she'd seen in the park. They'd stop in some shadowy place and then he'd touch her and kiss her and maybe more...

The people in front of her paused to admire the display outside one of the bookshops, so Maritsa stopped too. On the trestle table, books lay in heaps under swinging light bulbs: picture books and cheap paperbacks, serious-looking books with gold lettering on their spines, books for children and textbooks for students. Maritsa opened the most expensive-looking one and found it full of rude pictures of naked ladies – *gadjé* women, unclean – no good gypsy would allow herself to be seen like that. She gasped. She sniggered. But after a while, the rudeness wore off; after all, one lady with no clothes on was the same as another.

She picked up a children's book with large print and began mouthing all the words she knew. She felt proud of herself: she was *almost* reading. She looked at the price. If she wanted to, she could buy it. She took out a fistful of money; with money you had power, you could do anything. She pulled out a fifty-franc note and some coins, then stowed the rest away. Something else to hide from the boys, she thought. A book? A *kids'* book? Oh they'd get her for that, she'd never hear the end of it.

She picked up the book and wriggled through the crowd.

Behind the counter, the salesman prepared to pounce. Gypsies, he thought. Steal anything. Can't trust them an inch. Good thing I spotted this one.

'I want to buy this book please,' said Maritsa.

The man gulped: this business was full of surprises. He took the little parcel of money, checked the price, shook the coins into his hand, frowned at the note before stacking it in the till, then, shrugging, picked up the book and slipped it into a bag.

'For your little sister?' he asked awkwardly (while he concentrated on Maritsa, a man in a raincoat slipped a copy of PARIS BY NIGHT into his pocket and walked briskly away).

'None of your business,' said Maritsa, 'is it?'

After she left, she lovingly she ran her fingers over the brown-paper package. It was *her* book, her very own book. She could see herself opening it, smoothing down the pages. She looked up. It was late. The city sky was glowing black. She ought to go straight home, but what would they say? What would they do to her?

And she'd have to hide that book. She'd have to hide those shoes. Oh, she was a such a bad girl.

But she suddenly caught sight of her shoes again, twinkling in and out like two jewels on her feet. She had the most beautiful shoes in the world. And she owned a book, a proper book, and she'd made all that loot without even trying. Tomorrow she could make a lot more. By the end of the week she might have enough to pay for a little room and she could buy herself a plant in a pot and a songbird in a cage... Like a *gadjé* girl? She grinned. No, because inside she knew she was free. And if she got tired of being in one place, she could always change it for another...

Ahead of her she saw the sign for the next Métro station, but a side street smelt invitingly of fried sweetcorn and chips. Maritsa turned away from the big orange M. Later she would go back to it, but not to catch the train home. She knew now what she was going to do. The Métro was warm. You could sleep in the Métro. People did it all the time — beggars and drunks and old men who had nowhere else to go. Maritsa was streetwise, she knew how to be tough. And it wouldn't be for long — just until she'd made enough money...

It was a good street, a warm street, a street of food. Fragrant steam rose up from the hot-dog stall, and the little Arab sweet-shops were filled with pastel mounds of Turkish delight and coconut ice and crackly pastries sprinkled with pistachios and meringues as big as a baby's head.

A skinny boy was frying tiny yellow corncobs, turning them over and over with a long wooden fork. When he saw Maritsa watching him, he grinned, exposing a row of small, decaying teeth.

'Try one,' he invited, offering her one of the cobs.

It scorched her tongue but it tasted delicious. She smiled at him. It was easy to make friends.

Then customers arrived and at once he grew serious, taking money, giving change and carefully wrapping each cob in a square of greaseproof paper. Maritsa licked her fingers and tried to catch his eye but he was much too busy, so after a while she wandered away.

At the end of the street, the church of St Séverin, softly illuminated, was like a sugar house with windows of green-black ice. Maritsa found a stone ledge and sat down on it. Feeling very grand, she took out her book – really, she knew quite a lot of words. She played at stringing them into sentences, filling in the gaps with outrageous guesses.

After a while she became aware of someone watching her. She looked up and saw a boy in a black leather jacket holding a mobile phone.

'Want to come and eat with me, gypsy?'

Maritsa gasped. He was so handsome and he spoke so softly and he'd spoken to *her*.

Confused, she struggled up, clumsily pushing the book into its brown-paper bag. She didn't know what to do. Her cheeks were scarlet. In the shadows, someone sniggered.

The boy grabbed her arm and marched her down to one of the restaurants. Through windows frosted with imitation snow, Maritsa could see fairy lights and wine bottles lying in silver buckets and candles flickering on poppy-red cloths. She could imagine herself sitting at one of those tables, the waiter offering her a big, tasselled menu book – well, why not? she thought. Today anything could happen. Today was magic. Today was hers.

She turned to the boy, searching his good-looking face for kindness. Was this what had happened to her mother, long ago? Was this what had tempted her mama – pretty lights, pretty clothes and menu books with gold tassles? And she was her mother's daughter and just as wayward...

'Yes please,' she stammered.

The boy grinned triumphantly. He had never expected such a satisfying response.

Suddenly Maritsa could clearly see the mocking curve of his mouth and the cold sneer in his narrowing eyes.

'The gypsy and I are dining out tonight,' he called out, putting on an exaggerated accent.

Three other boys emerged from a doorway and strolled over. One of them posed with his hand on his heart.

'Could I have the honour tomorrow night?' His breath stank of booze.

The other two pushed him out of the way, laughing.
'Where shall we take you, princess? Maxim's? The Ritz?'

CHAPTER FOUR

Maritsa jerked herself free and began to run. The boys sniggered, enjoying her panic. She fled back down the street, prancing awkwardly in her high heels. Several times she stumbled.

When she reached the corncob stall she paused briefly and turned. The boys were still following her, not running, just strolling, just taking their time. She tried to catch the eye of the corn-cob seller, but he was hedged in by customers.

She turned the corner and ran down the Boulevard St Michel. Ahead, the big M for Métro glowed comfortingly. She took off her shoes, scuttled down the steps and, too panicky to fumble for her ticket, ducked under the barrier to save time. Along the passageway she stopped to slip on her shoes but already, behind her, she could hear them coming.

Still laughing, the boys had clattered down the steps and vaulted the barrier, one by one.

'Don't leave us, gypsy,' they called out.

Maritsa began running again.

'I fancy you, gypsy. Come and share your fleas with me!'

'Little gypsy slag!'

'Your eyes are like turds...'

'You smell like a pig. We love the way you smell. Don't go away...'

Maritsa ran on to a platform, diving and ducking through the crowd. The boys followed after. People backed away, making them a path. Yobs like that could turn violent, they said and after all, the girl was only a gypsy.

She reached the end of the platform and there was nowhere else to go. She begged the Blessed Virgin for a train but the good Lady wasn't listening.

The boys approached her slowly, savouring her terror. They had her cornered now, trapped like an animal. It amused them to frighten people. It turned them on, made them feel good. And beggars and gypsies were vermin, everyone knew that. Paris ought to be cleaned up.

Behind Maritsa, humped across three yellow plastic seats, lay a bundle of rags – a patchwork of grubby blue-printed tatters, a threadbare mess of grey and brown wool. From one end of this bundle protruded a pair of workman's boots, filthy and gaping with holes through which oozed lumps of matted beige sock. At the other end lay a green velvet hat, elaborately pleated and twisted and intricately shaped, out of which curled wisps of white hair.

Maritsa's right shoe suddenly swivelled sideways, throwing her off balance and she fell clumsily, hands first, tripping over two bulging carrier bags.

The bundle quivered and grunted and a voice complained, 'Leave my stuff alone!'

Maritsa stumbled back, turned round and there were the boys. She stared down at their feet, at the four pairs of trainers. She saw a knifeblade flicked out between thumbnail and finger and a ring with a swastika glittering on the hand. The studs on black leather were like iron sequins, were like nails in her coffin...

She heard a train approaching, but now it was too late. She tried to make a run for it but they were there before her, plucking at her hair.

'Just as I thought,' sneered one of them. 'Fleas.'

They pushed her down against the rags.

'Got one!' they sniggered.

'That one got away!'

'Look at the size of them!'

The train stopped and the doors to freedom slid open. Maritsa struggled and clawed but they pushed her back.

'Don't leave us yet, gypsy. We fancy you.'

'Sister-fuckers!' spat Maritsa in Rom.

The boys aped the sound, then laughed. 'She's a little Slav. Talks monkey. Can't understand French.'

'She's a little slag! Show us your tits, slag!'

'Call those tits? She hasn't got none...'

The good-looking boy grabbed her by the hair. 'Want to fuck me, fleabag?'

The others jeered. 'You'd have to disinfect yourself afterwards...'

The bundle of rags suddenly uncurled.

'Get on that train!' The voice was unexpectedly powerful.

The boys let go of Maritsa. This newcomer was a bonus.

'Smelly old hag!'

'Shut your ugly face, *grand-mère!*'

But the wrinkled finger jabbed fearlessly at their jackets. 'Get on that train!'

They backed away, brushing themselves. The old cow was probably diseased.

'Gypsy filth,' they muttered. 'Is she your grannie?'

The doors were already closing as they forced their way between them.

'Old pisspot!' they yelled as the train swept them away. Then they swaggered through the carriages, looking for new victims.

The two bags were shoved back and the rags collapsed again across the yellow plastic seats. The tattered blanket was pulled and tucked round the ragged blue cotton skirt; the boots became solid and immovable, like two black rocks. A grimy hand reached up to ease tufts of hair inside the green velvet hat and two bright eyes became just another couple of wrinkles.

Maritsa stared at the bundle in amazement. She put out her hand and patted it shyly. When this produced no response, she poked it with her finger. One watery grey eye opened.

'Thank you,' cried Maritsa. 'I thought they were going to kill me.'

The grey eye hazed and began to close.

Maritsa tried again.

'Thank you,' she said loudly. 'Thank you, *grand-mère.*'

The grey eye opened again. 'No need to shout. I'm not deaf.'

Maritsa giggled. 'You really gave them a fright!'

'Gave who a fright?'

'Those boys...'

The old woman burped deafeningly. 'Be off with you, gypsy kid. Go home. Leave me in peace.'

'I'm not going home.' Saying it boldly, like that, made Maritsa feel braver.

'Rubbish.'

'It's not rubbish. And I'm not a kid – I'm nearly thirteen. And I can manage just as well as you.'

'And your mother? What's she going to say?'

'Got no mother,' said Maritsa smugly.

The old woman sniffed.

'Well, your papa then. Bet he'll belt you!'

Maritsa smirked. 'My papa's too busy,' she said. 'Got important things to do. He's on TV,' she added casually.

'Who do you live with, then?'

Marista shrugged. 'People,' she said. 'Just some people.'

The old woman yawned, revealing sparse, jagged teeth. 'Please yourself,' she mumbled. 'No business of mine.' And scratching herself vigorously, she turned her head to the wall.

Maritsa squatted on the ground. The platform was beginning to fill up again. A couple stood pressed against the tiles, embracing passionately. She spied on them for a while, then she lost interest. She took out her book and looked at all the words. A train came in. One crowd was exchanged for another. Maritsa tried to construct a new story out of the words she knew. Beside her, the old woman had begun to snore.

She tucked the book away and began to think about Stefan and Nicolas, wondering what they were doing. They might have stinging bottoms from the mama's hefty smacks, but they'd have full stomachs, that was certain.

Wistfully she thought about the big evening fry-up. Maybe the mama had even baked some bread (French loaves were empty, thin, she always said, full of holes, not nourishing.) Outside someone would have started a bonfire and the kids would be fooling around between lines of frozen washing, yelling and scrambling over mounds of old tyres. There'd be the rich smell of thick black coffee brewing on the rusty gas burner and the constant comforting rhythm of the generator (could she sleep without it?).

And in the van, between tasselled lace curtains, the windows would be clouded with warm breath and loaded plates and cans of beer would be passed round the shiny plastic cloth with its big pink roses. And TV would be playing and babies who'd slept all day would suddenly get lively and one of the blokes might pick up a fiddle and the mama'd tap her feet and sway, putting her plump, sweaty arms around Maritsa and the boys...

She could still go back, she thought. Even now...

Trains came and trains went. The crowds grew thinner. Later there were just two or three people, sometimes none. The long empty platform was scary, eerie. The black 'O' of the tunnel became full of ghosts. Then Maritsa looked across at the old woman, sleeping like a baby. If an old grannie like that could do it, then so could she.

The doors of the last train closed and it moved away. Maritsa kicked off her shoes and pattered off to pee in the ladies toilet. When she got back, the shoes were still there where she'd left them. She picked them up and cradled them on her lap, running her fingers lovingly over the velvety suede and the silver crescent. It was the first real chance she'd had to admire them properly. They were exquisite. Beautiful. A pop star's shoes.

She wanted to show them off to someone.

'Look at my shoes,' she said, poking at the bundle of rags.

The old woman stirred irritably.

'No peace with you around, is there?' she complained. 'Go home. Go home to your mama.'

'I told you,' said Maritsa, 'I haven't got a mama and I'm not going home. And I'm sleeping down here tonight. With you.'

The old woman shrugged herself further into the blanket. 'Do what you please,' she mumbled. 'I can't stop you.'

Maritsa arranged herself against the wall. She wrapped the shoes in a fold of her skirt, tucked her book under her arm and resolutely closed her eyes. The ground was hard and cold. She put an arm under her head as a pillow. She was really very tired, she told herself. She could sleep anywhere. She'd drop off in a minute or two. Her arm started to ache. She opened her eyes and lay for a while staring up at the huge, glossy mouth of a woman on a poster. Above her, the soft mound heaved and subsided.

Maritsa made up her mind. She got up and curled herself across the two remaining seats, her head resting against the old woman's body. The rough blanket stank, but it was comforting and warm, like a smelly old cushion.

A small man in uniform walked slowly down the platform. When he reached the yellow plastic seats he stopped and poked at Maritsa.

'Station's closed, *mademoiselle*,' he said briefly. 'Can't sleep there.'

The old woman stirred and rolled over, pushing Maritsa off.

'You've acquired a visitor, Rose.' The man's voice was almost apologetic. 'I'm just moving her on.'

The old woman sat up.

'This is my granddaughter,' she announced firmly. 'She's staying with me.'

The man sighed. 'Rose, be sensible. That girl's a gypsy.'

The old woman looked angry. 'Who d'you think you are, Bertrand Leblanc,' she said, 'calling my grandchild a gypsy?' The man seemed to cower. 'I'll have you out of my class for rudeness. I won't stand for it! You know that!'

'Rose...'

The old woman sniffed. '*Mademoiselle* to you.'

'She can't stay.' The man's voice was pleading now. 'Can't you see that? I'll lose my job. I only let you sleep down here because of the weather.'

'I sleep down here,' said the old woman calmly, 'because I

choose to. And I will leave,' she added, 'whenever I choose to leave.' She sniffed. 'I've known far better places than this in my time, believe me...' And she rolled over and farted loudly.

The man glared at Maritsa. Then he shrugged and turned away.

'You'll leave when I tell you to go,' he muttered. The further he walked, the louder his voice became. 'First day of spring and out you'll go, old times' sake or not. Ungrateful old bag...'

CHAPTER FIVE

Maritsa couldn't believe it.

Granddaughter, she'd said. The old woman was crazy, mad as an owl, but *granddaughter?*

No one had ever claimed Maritsa before. The boys were always reminding her that they were not her real brothers, that the mama was not really Maritsa's mama but someone who, out of the goodness of her heart, had fostered an orphan. Kids were looked after by everyone, of course, but they still had families. And 'grandmother' was such a beautiful word. If you had a *grand-mère,* you really belonged, you had roots.

The old woman had settled down again, after fussing over her bags and pulling the blanket up over her head. Maritsa curled herself against her. 'Good night *Grand-mère,*' she said.

The old woman grunted, then began to breathe heavily. Maritsa waited for the snoring but it never came...

All at once, there was a clanging and a clashing of metal gates. Somebody whistled. Someone shouted, then laughed.

Maritsa opened her eyes sleepily and found that the lights were still on. She looked around, puzzled. Where was the heart-

beat rhythm of the generator? And where was the souvenir stat-
ue of St Sarah-la-Kali, with her flickering ruby lamp and her
waxy garlands? Where were the mirrors and the painted mer-
maid and the family photos in their big silver frame? And the
mama's tasselled gold cushions and the cuckoo clock and the
little TV on the shelf? She sat up, but all she could see was that
woman in the poster with her big glossy lips and her row of
white teeth.

Then she remembered — she was in the Métro. And of
course the light hadn't changed, but it was morning. She could
tell by the cleaners in their blue overalls and a little group of
immigrant workers patiently waiting for the first train.

She prodded the soft bundle she'd been lying against. 'It's
morning,' she cried.

The bundle shifted and gobbled.

She tried again. 'Wake up, *Grand-mère.*'

The old woman began to snore.

Maritsa put on her beautiful new shoes. She felt good. She'd
done it. She'd got away from those yobs and she'd slept all night
in the Métro. It was easy, she thought; nothing to it. And now
a train was coming. She could start working right away. If she
made an early start she'd get a lot of money...

But she was hungry.

She poked the old woman again; she couldn't just leave

without saying goodbye.

'I'm off now,' she said.

The old woman didn't move.

Then Maritsa remembered something. 'Bye, Rose,' she teased.

The old woman turned and looked at her crossly. 'Don't you get familiar with me, my girl.'

Maritsa giggled. 'Bye, *Grand-mère...*'

'*Grand-mère, grand-mère,*' grumbled Rose. 'I'm not your grannie. Be off with you.'

Maritsa hesitated for a moment. Then she walked away. At the exit, she turned and looked back for the last time. *Grand-mère,* she thought. Grandmother Rose. That sounded so pretty...

The early-morning Métro was different. There were no buskers in the passageways, no tourists, no moon-eyed lovers, no shopping ladies, no kids, no girls eyeing themselves critically in every reflective surface. Maritsa stood on the slatted step, slowly ascending past a few groups of workmen with sleep-glazed eyes and a couple of travellers stooped under rucksacks.

She fed her ticket through the machine and walked across the concourse. Up in the street, the air was icy, she could tell from the bar of frozen light that came zigzagging down the steps and the little gusts of cold that seemed to enter the place with each new passenger.

But inside the snack bar, coffee steamed fragrantly and the first croissants of the morning had just been delivered.

Maritsa bought herself croissants and a sandwich and a bowl of coffee. The woman behind the bar gave her a hard look.

'Don't you start your begging in my place,' she said, 'or I'll have you thrown out.'

But Maritsa scarcely heard. She took a mouthful of ham and lettuce, enjoying the melting butter, biting down into the warm crust of bread. She was crowing. She'd managed alone for a day and a night, she'd slept in the Métro and she still had money in her bag. She took out a fistful of coins and notes — easily enough for another sandwich, maybe two.

Then she began wondering where Rose would eat her breakfast, if Rose would have any breakfast. *Grand-mère*, she thought.

She bought a second sandwich. She looked at it hungrily: it was all she would have to eat until she'd made some more money — silly to give it away. Nevertheless she wrapped it in a paper napkin and carried it over to the down escalator.

But at the far end of the platform, the yellow plastic seats were empty now. Maritsa stood, looking down at them. Someone had wiped them clean, disinfected them and now they sat, all bright and shiny, like a row of polished yellow suns. She pushed away a vague feeling of loss. Who cared, after all? The old woman was nothing to her, a *gadji*, didn't even speak her language. She looked at the sandwich. She could save it for later. It would be good to have something to eat after she'd finished work.

A train came, its doors sliding open invitingly, but still Maritsa hesitated, reluctant to leave. Perhaps the old woman was wandering about outside. It was still early, she thought. She could afford to waste a few minutes looking – she might even make a franc or two.

The outer passageways were beginning to fill with office workers, brisk and snappy, intent on catching their early-morning trains. Maritsa smoothed out her note and offered it, but the sandwich in its paper napkin wrecked her image and anyway they'd seen plenty of her kind before.

Somewhere ahead, a thin, warbling sound rose and fell. A morning drunk? thought Maritsa. Some nutcase? And she followed the sound to find out.

The old woman sat crouched against the tiled wall. She wore the ragged brown blanket round her shoulders like a cape and her knees were two bumps under a heavy tweed skirt.

'...*Quand il me prend dans ses bras...*' she wailed, one wrinkled hand thrust aggressively under the noses of passers-by. Around her, scattered, lay half a dozen centimes thrown by some joker.

Marista burst out laughing and the warbling stopped.

The old woman glared at her. 'What are you laughing at?'

'You,' choked Maritsa. 'You've got such an awful voice!' She looked over the money. 'How much do you make doing that?'

Rose regarded her sourly. 'Enough,' she said. 'Thought I'd got rid of you,' she added. 'Thought you'd gone home to your mama.'

'Told you.' Maritsa felt smug. 'I'm not going to.' She squatted down beside Rose and held out the sandwich. 'Got you some breakfast,' she said.

The old woman stared. Then she made a grab for the sandwich and bit into it, turning her head sideways like a puppy and worrying at it with her few remaining teeth. When she'd finished, she wiped her mouth with the back of her hand and brushed the crumbs from her stained silk. Then she burped.

'Oh, shut up!' giggled Maritsa.

Rose looked offended. 'Don't you be rude, my girl.'

They sat for a while, watching people pass.

'What's inside those bags?' asked Maritsa curiously.

'None of your business,' said Rose. 'Just leave them alone.'

Maritsa had an idea. 'Show you something,' she said. She took off her shoes and tucked them in behind Rose, covering them with a fold of fabric. This was going to be good. This was going to be really good.

She held out her hand.

'Money for my gran,' she whined. 'Give me something for my poor old gran. My gran's not well. Hasn't eaten for days. Ought to see the doctor but she can't afford to. Money for my gran. Please help my gran.'

One or two of the punters began to linger; there was something about the sight of a child protecting an old woman that got to them.

Rose started to protest. 'Lies. All lies,' she grumbled. 'She *can't* be my grandchild, she's a gypsy, can't you see?'

The little pile of coins began to grow, but Rose ignored it.

'Girl's a fibber,' she growled. 'I'm not her grannie.'

'Oh, shut up!' Maritsa whispered urgently, 'you silly old cow!' Then she called out to the passers-by: 'Help my poor old gran! Please help my gran.'

'I'm not her gran,' argued Rose and somebody sniggered. 'Do I *look* like her gran?' And somebody laughed.

After an hour or so of this, Maritsa gave up. She was tired and hoarse and sick of trying to fight against Rose's heckling. She scooped up the money and slipped it into her pouch. For once, Rose was silent. Maritsa glanced sideways and found her asleep, her head on one side and her mouth all askew.

She put on her shoes. 'I'm off,' she announced crossly.

The old woman opened one eye. At once, Maritsa felt guilty. 'OK, I'll go shares,' she offered. 'I couldn't have done it without you. But why didn't you belt up? You nearly spoilt the whole show.'

Rose sniffed. 'I don't hold with lies.'

'We were working,' said Maritsa. 'That doesn't count.'

'Call that work?' exclaimed Rose. 'You don't know what work is, my girl.'

Maritsa quickly changed the subject. 'I can read,' she said proudly. She sat down again. 'I've got a book. Want to see my book?' and she took it out of its bag and slipped it on to the old woman's lap.

Rose glanced at it irritably and pushed it aside. Then she dragged over one of the bags. She fumbled about, then drew out a tiny pair of metal-rimmed spectacles and placed them shakily half-way down her nose, looping the spidery wires around her ears. Then she reached for the book. She opened it at the first page. Maritsa's eyes were round with disbelief.

'THE STORY OF CINDERELLA,' she read. She looked at Maritsa over the tops of her spectacles. 'Aren't you a bit old for this sort of thing?'

'It's for my sister,' lied Maritsa. 'My little sister.'

'More lies,' accused Rose. She handed it back. 'Let me hear you read it.'

'OK,' said Maritsa. She pointed at the words but she looked at the pictures. 'This girl is sweeping the floor.' She turned over the page. 'That lady's her boss.'

Rose snorted. 'That's not reading...' She took the book back again. 'ONCE UPON A TIME...'

'You can read?' said Maritsa. 'Just like that?'

The old woman shrugged. 'Anyone can read,' she said. 'A big girl like you – you should know your letters.'

But Maritsa was working something out. 'You can write too?'

'Naturally.'

'Then between us we'll make a packet! Listen. Just stay there. Don't move. Don't go away. I'll be back.'

Rose suddenly caught sight of Maritsa's shoes.

'Who do you think you are, girl?' she said. 'The Queen of England?' She pointed at her own heavy boots with their tangle of laces. 'Look at these. Solid leather. Best quality. Lasted me for years, these boots.'

'You're just jealous,' called Maritsa. She walked to the end of the passageway and rode up on the escalator. She slipped her ticket through the machines, pushed open the swing doors and ran up the steps to the street. Outside, cold iced her cheeks and her warm breath clouded the air.

Close to the exit was a stationer's shop, its windows full of gift sets of coloured pencils and felt-tipped pens. Maritsa went inside, picked up a packet of blackboard chalks, handed over her one franc coin, and walked back to the Métro.

Along the passageway, she could hear Rose singing again. Maritsa caught up with her.

'Look what I've got,' she said.

Rose stopped singing to examine the chalks.

'Don't want them,' she said at last. 'I've retired. I told you.'

Maritsa grinned. Then she kicked off her shoes and squatted on the floor. She shook out the coloured chalks and chose a pink one. Remembering the look of the letters, she began to write:

MY MUTHER AN FATHER ARE DED. She remembered how to make the words up from the note. Then she added something new: I LIV WIV MY GRAN. MY GRAN IS ILL. WE DO NOT HAV ENNY FOOD.

'Rubbish,' said Rose. 'We've just eaten.'

'You'll see...'

'Pack of gypsy lies.'

'Oh, don't start all that again,' said Maritsa. 'We'll make piles of money. Watch.'

One or two people paused to read the message on the floor.

'It's not true,' Rose informed them. She pointed at Maritsa. 'I'm not her gran. She made it all up.' Somebody laughed.

'Anyway,' she added, 'the gypsy can't spell.'

Maritsa had had enough. She'd done her best. Now the old woman could starve for all she cared.

'Rotten old witch!' she shouted. 'Lousy old bat! Let's see you do it, then,' and she threw a handful of chalks into the old woman's lap.

Rose dragged herself round. She tut-tutted over the uneven letters. Then she looked at Maritsa and shook her head. 'Shame on you, girl!' She began scrubbing at the mispelt words with the palms of her hands.

A little crowd began to gather, enjoying the spectacle.

'Go on, grannie,' someone shouted. 'Teach her!'

'I will,' said Rose fiercely. 'I will.'

She began to rewrite the message. A few coins came rolling over the letters and once or twice, a note came floating down. When she'd finished, she crawled back and squatted against the wall. Someone laughed and called out, '*Bravo, la mamie!*'

'If you've got to tell lies,' Rose declared, 'at least spell them right.'

The crowd clapped and cheered and threw more coins.

Maritsa gathered them up but her eyes were on Rose. 'Teach me,' she pleaded. 'Will you?'

Rose shoved her fingers under the green velvet hat and scratched vigorously. 'Big girl like you not knowing her letters,' she grumbled. 'Don't they send you to school?'

Maritsa pulled a face. 'Schools don't want us,' she said. 'And we don't want them. We know enough, we know plenty, more than you...' She pounded on Rose's bulky thigh. 'You teach me.'

Rose sighed. She pointed at the rewritten message. 'Copy it,' she ordered. 'That's how people learn.'

'Good for you, *grand-mère*,' someone shouted.

'That's right, teach her!'

'Teach her to keep her off the trains.'

'Or the streets...'

Painstakingly Maritsa copied out the letters. Changing the colour, she wrote them out again. Then she tried writing each word in a different hue.

Rose watched, nodding approvingly. 'Application,' she said primly. Then her eyelids grew heavy and her face sagged. She shuddered and the pudding-basin hat slipped down over her eyes. Soon she started to snore. Bored, the crowd melted away.

Maritsa prodded her.

'Give me another word. I know all these.'

Rose gazed at her dopily through half-open eyes.

'More words,' said Maritsa.

'Practice,' said Rose vaguely, 'makes perfect.' She yawned.

'What's that supposed to mean?' asked Maritsa, but Rose was asleep again.

Maritsa shrugged. She drew a pattern on the ground and coloured it orange and green. She drew a pink flower and gave it a yellow centre. She drew a face with crossed eyes and sticking-out teeth. Then she stamped on the chalk. 'I'm hungry,' she said.

There was no reply.

'I'm hungry!' she yelled.

Rose jumped out of her sleep. 'Eat then,' she said.

'What about you?'

'I can take care of myself. Not like some.'

'But we've got money!'

'Your lies, your money.'

Maritsa sighed. She tipped out a handful of coins and wrapped them in a note. Then she threw the little parcel into Rose's lap. 'Your share,' she said.

Rose sniffed.

Maritsa hesitated. 'Bye then...'

Rose pointed and cackled. 'Silly shoes!'

'I might come back later.'

'Don't bother,' said Rose. 'Leave me in peace. And get your-self some sensible boots,' she called after Maritsa. 'Catch your death!'

Maritsa turned and stuck out her tongue.

Then she walked away.

CHAPTER SIX

At the foot of the escalators, the homeless woman's daughter was begging inexpertly, thrusting her hand under people's chins and repeating, like a mantra, 'Change, spare change.' When she spotted Maritsa she thumbed her nose. 'Gypsy!' she yelled.

Maritsa spat, aiming at the nice blue hand-knitted jumper. Then she rode up, pushed through the barrier and walked across the concourse. Outside the snack bar, she hesitated. Another sandwich? Or a *brioche*? Maybe even a *Croque-Monsieur.* Then she saw sunlight dancing down the steps and remembered yesterday's pancake feast in the Luxembourg Gardens.

She went up and out, hurrying past the side street where she'd lingered last night. The fragrances of the food stalls were still seductive, but the faces of those boys were too fresh in her mind. She dawdled over bookshops and papershops, goggled at paintings through a gallery window, picked out clothes for herself from an expensive *boutique and* riffled through a street trader's banner of scarves for so long that their thin silver flocking came off on her hands. When he chased her away, she zigzagged through the traffic with a crowd of students and stepped once again through the big iron gates.

Hearing a vague sound of music, she walked, still wobbling slightly in her new shoes, past statues and skeleton trees, clipped evergreens, shaved lawns rimmed with little hedges and stone fountains switched off for the winter. Her feet were rubbed and blistered now but she didn't care. The shoes, as she watched them, were jewels, were violets, were two purple plums with a silvery bloom. *Her* shoes...

Hers?

She wondered if those photographers would be there today, if that model lady would see what Maritsa was wearing and call out, 'Thief! Thief!' But the park was big and she'd see them coming. Anyway, they were her shoes now; they always had been. And anyway, it wasn't really stealing; she knew the story. God allowed gypsies a small share in *gadjé* treasure, for hadn't it been a gypsy who'd hidden baby Jesus in a basket when Herod was looking for Him? The Blessed Virgin had probably *made* that lady throw those shoes on the step...

When she reached the sandy terrace where the pancake stall stood, she found a carousel with fairy lights and painted horses on barley-sugar poles and mirrors that twinkled and winked in the sun. Maritsa bought herself a hot dog and a couple of pancakes and sat down on a bench to watch. Once, long ago, someone had lifted her on to a carousel much grander than this one, with loud music and horses that swung out so far that she'd screamed. But then she'd been a kid, then she'd been little. Girls of twelve didn't ride on painted horses.

So what? She still looked like a kid or she couldn't have worked the Métro. She could do what she liked.

She climbed on, chose a horse and arranged herself modestly, side-saddle, spreading her skirts. Who cared? It was fun. Anyway, she could pay.

And in the shadow of the bushes, somebody moved.

The showman spotted her. 'Off with you, gypsy!'

'But I can pay,' protested Maritsa, showing him her money.

'Get off my machine or I'll call the cops!'

A man in a green padded jacket stepped out of the shadows. He walked up to the carousel and waved something at the showman. 'Let the kid stay,' he said. A camera swung from his plump neck.

The showman eyed the wad of notes. 'If you say so, *monsieur*. But it's against the rules. That gypsy kid's eleven if she's a day and they're supposed to be ten or under.' He held out his hand. 'Could get me into a load of trouble...' But he smiled as he slipped the money into his black leather bag.

Another photographer, thought Maritsa warily, but nothing to do with yesterday's model lady. Paris was full of photographers. This one was just a funny, nice man.

But was he?

She checked as he came round again and again – the pale, heavy face, the reddish brush of a moustache, the two black reflective mirrors concealing the eyes.

He stepped back and crouched. The camera focused on her.

Why her? she wondered.

Maybe he was a police spy, come to photograph the evidence. There it was, after all, on her two feet.

The man lay down on his back. He seemed to be concentrating on her shoes. Guiltily, Maritsa swung sideways, hiding them under her skirts, but the man only laughed. 'Don't be shy, *mademoiselle!*'

The carousel slowed and stopped. Maritsa tried to make a run for it but he was there, waiting for her.

The game was up, she thought.

She slipped off the shoes and held them out.

The man looked puzzled. 'I don't want your shoes.' Then he seemed to catch on. 'They aren't yours, are they?'

The showman nodded approvingly. 'That's right, *monsieur*. You nab her. Pinch anything, these gypsy kids.'

Maritsa suddenly felt sick. 'I didn't really steal them,' she pleaded. 'I found them.' She pointed. 'Over by the lake. On the steps.'

The man took a bag of sweets out of his pocket. 'You'd

better come along with me,' he said. He unwrapped a caramel cream. 'Have one?'

But Maritsa was staring at his camera, wanting to grab it and smash out all those images of herself, all those bits of her soul that cop had stolen away.

'Put your shoes back on,' he was saying. He spoke French with a funny accent. 'OK, kid, let's go.'

She had no choice, Maritsa thought. No point in lying now. Oh, how she hated policemen, how she hated cops. 'Prison?' she whispered.

The man nodded grimly.

'How long?'

The man stopped and considered. 'Depends on the judge...' She watched his jaws working on the caramel. 'Ten, twenty years probably, since you're a gypsy. Serious crime. Must be worth a packet, those shoes.'

Maritsa was shocked. She'd be grown up. She'd be old. And they'd question her, maybe beat her – the cops would use any excuse to get rid of a gypsy, she knew that. They might go to Gennevilliers, raid the camp and bring in the mama and the boys. And they'd want to know where she'd spent the night, they might even pick up Rose...

She tried not to cry. Only little kids cried.

She fought against the tears but the man noticed.

He looked alarmed. 'Don't start blubbering here!' Then he seemed to recover. 'Come and sit down, *mademoiselle*.' He slid an arm round her shoulders. 'You're upset. I scared you.' He unwrapped another sweet and popped it into his mouth. 'Listen,' he said thickly. 'I was teasing. I'm not really a cop.'

Maritsa stared at him dumbly.

'Why do you think I took all those pics?' He put his face close to hers. His breath smelt of warm chocolate. 'I'm a film producer,' he confided. 'And I'm looking for someone just like you.'

Maritsa got up. He wasn't a cop. He'd said he wasn't a cop.

She tested him, stumbling away and he didn't do a thing. She slowed down and walked and he didn't come after her. She relaxed. He'd been a con man, she thought. Just a stupid con man. Enjoyed scaring people, that was all. And she scolded herself for being taken in, she, a gypsy, who should have been up to all the tricks.

She crossed the road by the subway and then she remembered. A film producer, he'd said; that was probably a lie too. Oh, if only he'd really been a film producer, she thought. He might have made her into a TV star, given her diamond earrings and one of those slinky sequinned dresses and books and magazines and all the shoes she'd ever wanted, all the shoes in the world...

She hesitated in front of a window full of cakes. Sweet things she *loved*. And there were chocolate eclairs and strawberry tarts. There were madeleines and marzipan fruits and Florentines and custard tarts. So who cared about being a star? These things were real and she could have them right now.

And inside the shop there were more treasures – sticky *palmiers* and spice breads, glazed triangles of apple pie and meringues as light and puffy as clouds.

A lady in a print overall was curling gold ribbons with the edge of a knife. *'Mademoiselle?'*

Maritsa pointed at a coffee-coloured meringue. 'One of those, please.'

'Only one?' Someone had moved in behind her. 'I'll pay for whatever the young lady chooses, *madame*.' Maritsa turned and there was the man from the park. She suddenly felt triumphant. He knew he'd scared her. OK, if he wanted to make amends, she'd give him something to pay for.

'And four strawberry tarts and four Florentines.' Maritsa eyed him, but he didn't look bothered.

The lady picked up the cakes with a pair of silver tongs and arranged them carefully inside two cardboard boxes. 'Anything else, *mademoiselle*?'

'Oh yes,' said Maritsa. 'I'll have some marzipan mice...' She suddenly felt rich and powerful. She considered the custard tarts. They were soft, easy to eat, and she wondered if Rose had had any lunch. 'And two custard tarts please.'

The man took out his wallet and paid the bill.

Maritsa picked up the two boxes and walked proudly out of the shop. She would keep the gold ribbon, she thought, to weave into her plaits. She sighed. This was how it must feel all the time, being a star.

'Don't I get a nice thank-you?' The man had caught up with her. He began fiddling with her hair. Maritsa instinctively moved away.

The man looked cross. 'That's not very friendly,' he complained, 'after all those cakes.'

'OK. Thank you,' said Maritsa coldly.

He fell into step beside her. 'You pigging up that lot your-self?'

'Not your business.'

'You'll be sick!' He stopped and held out his hand. 'Friends?'

Maritsa looked up at him. His grasp was firm and his mouth pink and smiley, but you couldn't be friends with a man with no eyes.

They walked down to the Métro station.

'You don't want to go down into that awful black hole,' said the man. 'A pretty little girl like you. I've got a car...'

'My gran lives down there,' said Maritsa quickly, 'She'll be waiting for me.'

The man shrugged.

'Well, it's up to you. I'll have to find someone else to star in my film. There are plenty of other girls. And there's money in it, my kids don't want for a thing. Tell your little friends. Name's Wilhelm. I'll be hanging out for the next few days in the Café Laure, round the back of the park. Auditioning. Early evenings. Change your mind, come and see me.'

'OK,' said Maritsa. 'And thank you for the cakes,' she repeated.

Wilhelm gave a stiff little bow. 'My pleasure...'

Maritsa ran down the steps and across the concourse. She could do it, she could do it, she *knew* she could do it. Money. Fame. Oh, she'd make the boys goggle when they switched on TV. A star, she thought. I could be a star.

She clicked through the barrier and stepped on to the escalator. Yet Wilhelm was not a good man, she thought. She could sense it, she could feel it. A man who hid his eyes, who took pictures without asking, what else might he take? She knew the score — there were one or two girls in the *kumpania* who'd been used by bad *gadjé* at home...

So what? Luck could be cruel and it might be a chance worth risking. She could take care of herself, couldn't she? Scratch, bite, spit, kick? And hadn't she slept all night in the Métro?

A little boy with a streaming nose went pumping beside her, running against the escalator and the homeless woman's daughter was still standing there, begging.

When Maritsa walked past her, she pulled a face.

'Gypsy,' she hissed. 'Filthy gypsy!'

Maritsa didn't care. She hugged the two boxes with their curly gold ribbons and began looking out for Rose. Their morning pitch had been taken over by an old man with a mouth organ, dribbling and wagging his head as he played, his bright eyes observing the passers-by. Maritsa felt for a coin and threw it on to his blanket. A star, she thought, could afford to be generous.

She walked past a lute player and a Bible man on a crate, climbed down the steps and there, at the end of the platform, she found the familiar bundle of rags. The old woman was sleeping like a baby, cheeks flushed, velvet hat squashed sideways against the yellow plastic seat.

Maritsa touched her shoulder. 'Rose?'

The old woman didn't move.

Maritsa poked her. '*Grand-mère?*'

Rose muttered and blinked.

'Got you some cakes.' Maritsa undid the ribbons and opened one of the boxes. 'Look.'

The old woman wrinkled her nose. 'What's all that stuff?'

'Custard tarts.'

The old woman sat up. 'Never thought much of custard tarts,' she remarked, reaching for one greedily.

Maritsa suddenly remembered something.

'Did you bring back my book?'

'What book?'

'My reading book.'

Rose sniffed. 'Big girl like you ought to take care of her own books.'

'Did you put it in one of your bags?' said Maritsa. 'Can I look?'

'You leave my bags alone.'

'Then give me my book. Give it to me,' Maritsa teased, 'or I won't give you any more cakes.'

'Rude,' muttered Rose. She fumbled in one of the bags and brought out the Cinderella book. 'Go back to where you belong,' she said. 'I'm not having any gypsies in my class.'

'Thank you, *Grand-mère.*'

Rose scowled. 'And I'm not your gran.' She held up the custard tart and examined it, turning it over and over in her hands. 'Never did think much of custard tarts,' she repeated, gnawing at it messily.

Maritsa squatted down beside her and started on a meringue. 'I met a man,' she said. A train thundered in.

Suddenly the platform was full of people. 'He makes films,' shouted Maritsa, her skirts full of sugary crumbs. 'Big American films. For TV.'

Rose helped herself to another custard tart.

'It was him who bought us the cakes,' yelled Maritsa. 'He's going to give me one of those screen tests. I could be a star.' Rose just went on eating. 'Don't you care?' asked Maritsa. A blob of custard tart slopped over the old woman's blouse. 'Ugh!' said Maritsa, picking it off with her fingers. 'You're disgusting! You're horrible!'

Rose adjusted her hat. 'No manners,' she said haughtily. 'No breeding. Anyone can tell you're only a gypsy.'

'Well, I'm going to be a star,' said Maritsa grandly. 'I'm going to have a posh apartment on the Champs Elysées, with a songbird in a cage and one of those big TVs. I might let you visit me if you behave.'

'I never go visiting,' sniffed Rose. 'I'm content where I am, thank you very much, not like you lot, always moving, always shifting, never satisfied. Travellers...' She settled down again.

Maritsa tucked into two of the strawberry tarts. She considered a third, but she felt fat and full.

The boxes were still only half empty.

She prodded Rose. 'Want another cake?'

But the old woman snorted and turned away, drawing the

blanket up over her head.

Grumpy old bag, thought Maritsa. There are plenty of other people who'd like one of those cakes and she topped up the second box with the rest of the tarts. Then she went for a walk. She was bored with Rose.

She offered the box to the old man with the mouth organ. He stared at it in disbelief and stopped playing. 'For me?'

Maritsa nodded.

His bony fingers shook as they lifted out a strawberry tart. 'You're a good little girl,' he told her. 'Really nice.'

She popped one inside the collecting hat of the Bible man. The Bible man lost his place in his holy book. He looked from the cake to Maritsa, then back to the cake. Then he stooped and picked out a strawberry. 'The woman tempted me, O Lord,' he cried. He pointed at Maritsa. 'That child of the Devil!'

'No, I'm not.' Maritsa grinned. 'My dad's a bishop, so there.'

She offered the box to the homeless woman who sat dumbly begging in the niche near the escalators.

The woman looked suspicious. 'Where did those come from?'

'They're a present,' said Maritsa. 'Someone gave them to me.'

The woman checked them over. 'Are they fresh?'

Maritsa nodded. 'Got them today.'

The woman sighed. 'People give you rubbish sometimes.

Just because I've got the kids down here doesn't mean I don't care. I've still got my pride.' She looked fiercely at Maritsa. 'But what would *you* know about that?'

The pink-cheeked girl who'd been begging came over.

'What's the gypsy giving you?' she asked, running her fingers through her short blonde hair.

'Have one,' said Maritsa. She picked out a marzipan mouse for the small boy who'd been running up the escalator, but the girl snatched it out of his hands. 'It's probably rotten,' she said.

Maritsa was furious. 'No, it's not.'

The girl looked over the rest of the cakes. 'I wouldn't touch them,' she said. Then she bit the head off the marzipan mouse.

The little boy screamed until Maritsa gave him the second mouse.

The girl glowered. 'You think you're smart, don't you?' she said. 'Well, you're not. You can't be — cos you're only a gypsy.'

The woman looked embarrassed. 'She's a nice gypsy, Sylvie,' she said. 'She's brought us these cakes.'

But the girl stared coldly at Maritsa.

'She's a stupid gypsy,' she repeated. '*And* she spits.'

CHAPTER SEVEN

On her way back, Maritsa met Rose, wading along the passage-way with her two precious bags.

Maritsa was amused. 'Where are you off to, *Grand-mère?*'

'None of your business,' said Rose coyly. She sidled up to the door marked LADIES.

Maritsa tried to help but Rose shook her head.

'I can manage perfectly well, thank you,' she said.

Maritsa hung about outside. She waited and waited. She could have picked up a few more francs, she thought, if it had-n't been for the cake box with its ribbons and those flashy shoes.

Rose came shuffling out.

'Let's get some more money,' Maritsa said. 'It was good this morning.'

The old woman said nothing.

'Shall we do it again?'

Rose frowned. 'Pack of lies you told.'

'Shall we do it now?' said Maritsa. 'Get some extra money for a nice supper?' She suddenly longed for a proper hot meal, the steaming cookpot, the mama's good cabbage stew with car-away dumplings.

'If I need people's charity,' declared Rose haughtily, 'I can ask for it myself.'

Three girls exaggeratedly side-stepped around them in a wave of perfume, giggling and holding their noses.

'Pooh!' they said.

'That old bag doesn't half pong!'

Maritsa made a rude gesture and spat and they moved disgustedly away. 'Dirty gypsy,' they called from a safe distance. 'Gypsy trash!'

Maritsa ignored them. She'd heard it all before.

'Here's a good pitch,' she said. 'Right here.' Suddenly she seized Rose's blanket and spread it out on the ground.

'Mine!' cried Rose. 'Gypsy thief, got no business...'

Still grumbling, she eased herself down, fussing over her skirt, tucking in her blouse and straightening her hat. Maritsa removed her shoes and stood for a while, thinking. Then she took out the chalk box and wrote the message: MY GRAN IS SICK... She rubbed out several letters with the palm of her hand and rewrote them, trying to get the right spelling. When she finished she looked slyly across at Rose to see if she'd noticed but already the old women had fallen asleep.

Maritsa tucked her shoes behind Rose's mass. Then she straddled the message, showing off her grubby, blistered feet (*Bare feet*, they'd exclaim, *and in the middle of winter...*)

Rose stirred and woke up. She yawned, blinked and adjusted her hat. Then she threw back her head and began to sing.

Maritsa was cross. A sick granny didn't sing. 'Be quiet,' she ordered, 'you're spoiling everything,' but Rose was lost in her own music.

Her wavering voice rose to a high, off-key treble. *'Love,'* she warbled, and *'Moonlight'* and *'Kisses'.*

Suddenly the passageway was filled with another sound. A man in a beige zipped jacket and a baseball cap had been setting up an act with a sound box and an electric guitar and already he was attracting quite a little crowd. This wasn't begging, people reasoned, this was entertainment; it was only right that he should be paid. Those two dumb beggars did nothing at all and still expected to be fed...

Maritsa gave up. She squatted down beside Rose. They would make little more until he moved so there really was no point in trying.

She took out the book. 'Teach me some more words,' she shouted, but Rose just went on singing soundlessly, her faltering voice drowned by heavy American rock.

Maritsa picked a word and chalked it out, deliberately misspelling it.

After a while, Rose glanced sideways at what she'd done.

She frowned and stopped singing. 'That's all wrong,' she said.

Maritsa grinned secretly and rubbed it out. 'Then you show me.' She tossed a piece of chalk into the old woman's lap.

And Rose was caught. 'This is the right way,' she said, shuffling forward and carefully chalking out the word in big looped writing.

'You write so well,' sighed Maritsa. 'I'll never be as good as you.'

'Application,' said Rose smugly.

'You said that before,' grumbled Maritsa. 'What's it mean?'

'It means trying hard,' said Rose. 'It means never giving up.'

Maritsa copied word after word. She even forgot to beg. Occasionally someone would comment on the strange lesson.

'Is that a game?'

'You teaching the gypsy kid to write?'

'Come back to my place, little gypsy,' breathed a middle-aged man, 'and I'll give you some more interesting lessons...'

The homeless woman's daughter turned up, with her small brother in tow. They stood, watching for a while.

'You can't teach gypsies,' declared the girl. 'They're stupid.'

Rose looked up. 'Take that little boy along to Infants,' she ordered. 'At *once!*'

The girl gaped at Maritsa. 'She potty?'

'She's my gran,' said Maritsa firmly. 'She's all right.'

The girl stroked her blue woolly jumper. '*My* gran's clever,' she boasted. 'She knitted me this.'

'That's nothing,' said Maritsa. 'Mine's teaching me to read,' The girl looked scornful. 'Can't you read yet?'

'Of course I can.' Maritsa showed her the book.

The girl laughed. 'Cinderella? That's kids' stuff.' She unrolled a tatty copy of MARIE CLAIRE and began turning the pages.

Maritsa looked with despair at the blocks of tiny print.

The girl squatted beside her. 'I'll show you the pictures if you like,' she offered haughtily, 'since you can't read,' and she flipped through the pages of fashion photos. '*Proper* people's clothes,' she explained smugly. 'Not for you. Not for gypsies.' And she undid her hairclip and shook out her straight blonde hair.

Rose suddenly reached over and seized the magazine. 'Not in *my* class,' she bellowed. The girl opened her mouth. 'I don't allow magazines.'

'But I'm not in your class,' the girl protested.

Rose looked puzzled for a moment. Then she pointed. 'In that case, off you go.' She gave the magazine back. 'And take this rubbish with you. Insulting my granddaughter,' she muttered.

The girl's cheeks went even pinker.

'Keep it,' she said, throwing it down. 'Give it to your gypsy kid. I wouldn't touch it after you, you smelly old bag.' She hauled her brother to his feet. 'We're going, Marcel.'

'Piss off!' yelled Maritsa. 'And don't come back!'

After an hour or so, the man in the beige zipped jacket packed up his gear and came over.

'I'm sorry. I spoilt your pitch,' he said.

Maritsa was surprised; buskers didn't usually say sorry for things like that. She looked up at him, puzzled. 'That's OK,' she said. He was cool, she decided – tall and hunky, with green-grey eyes and reddish-brown stubble.

'She really your gran?' he asked, looking at the sleeping Rose.

Maritsa nodded, admiring his Nike trainers.

'She OK?'

Maritsa shrugged. 'She's just old.'

'She eaten?'

Maritsa shook her head firmly.

'Want to eat with me? The two of you? Upstairs in the snack bar? To make up for spoiling your pitch?'

It seemed too good to be true, but you never knew with the *gadjé*, with their false, good-looking faces and their empty promises. But this bloke was a busker, a beggar, not so different from her. And if things turned nasty, there were two of them this time.

Maritsa pounded on Rose. '*Grand-mère*,' she yelled. Rose woke up with a start. 'We're going to eat.' She pointed. 'With him,' she added proudly.

Rose belched. 'Not hungry,' she muttered. 'And I never eat with strangers.'

'They make a very good onion soup up there,' the man said slyly. 'With *croûtons* and cheese...'

'And you *like* soup, don't you?' Maritsa added persuasively.

Tempted, the old woman struggled to her feet. The man tried to help her but she shook him off furiously. 'Just because I'm old,' she objected, 'there's no reason to take liberties!'

They walked past the homeless woman with her pencilled placard tied around her neck and the homeless woman's daughter with her little brother, begging at the foot of the stairs.

The man dropped a ten-franc coin into the girl's outstretched palm.

Maritsa threw her a superior glance. 'We're going out,' she said airily. 'To eat. In a *restaurant*.'

'Some restaurant,' sniffed the girl, 'if they let you in.'

They eased Rose on to the escalator, Maritsa holding her hand and the busker dumping his equipment and pushing from behind. 'Get your hands off me, young man,' bellowed Rose, 'or I'll call a cop.'

Maritsa began to giggle and once the giggle had started it

was impossible to stop. She giggled when they eased Rose's bulk off the escalator and she giggled all the way to the snack bar.

The snack bar chairs were small and delicate. Rose knocked one over. The man righted it but she knocked it over again. Maritsa went on giggling. Heads began to turn and the woman behind the bar shrugged, then sighed loudly.

The man unslung his guitar and propped it against the sound box, while Maritsa finally settled Rose, still grumbling, on to a chair. He went over to the bar and bought hot soup and sandwiches, then pulled up an extra table and returned for more. Maritsa spooned up her soup so fast that she burped.

Rose tut-tutted. 'Manners,' she complained.

The man held out his hand. 'The name's Paul.'

'I'm Maritsa,' said Maritsa. 'She's Rose.'

'*Mademoiselle* to strangers,' corrected Rose haughtily.

'Where do you sleep?' asked Paul.

'In the Métro, of course,' said Maritsa proudly.

'With your gran? No parents? No mother? No father?'

'I ran away,' explained Maritsa. 'My gran was kind, so I took her with me.' She remembered the story of the wicked step-mother. 'My real mum is dead and I lived with my stepmother. She beat me up. She made me do all the work. She wouldn't even let me go to the...' She stopped herself in time.

Paul looked sympathetic.

'Did they beat up your grannie too?'

Maritsa nodded solemnly but Rose looked furious.

'She's lying again,' she said. 'No one ever lays a hand on me. She's a gypsy and I'm not her grannie. I'm not anyone's grannie.' She slurped up her soup, then looked around. 'Been to *much* better places than this,' she remarked, blotting her mouth delicately with the hem of her blouse. 'High-class restaurants. Silver service. Champagne. Flowers...'

Maritsa was shocked. 'You mean old thing,' she exclaimed. 'You ought to be grateful. You ought to say thank you.'

'Doesn't matter. I owed you.' Paul took out a cigarette and lit it. 'That fair girl,' he said. 'She one of your friends?'

'*Her?*' Maritsa was amazed. 'She's horrible!'

Paul breathed out a thin veil of smoke. 'Are there many kids on this line?'

'How would I know?' said Maritsa. 'I don't hang around with kids.'

'Are you sure they won't come looking for you,' said Paul, 'your stepmother, your family? They won't be concerned?' He flicked off a stub of ash. 'And what if they're moved on?'

Maritsa suddenly felt uncomfortable, thinking of the lies she'd told about the mama and hating the way the *gadjé* talked about gypsies as if they weren't really people, as if they were just rubbish that had to be shifted.

'My lot could find me if they chose,' Maritsa said defiantly. 'And anyway I'm working by myself now. But only for a short time, then I'll be leaving...' She ran her fingers longingly over the top of the guitar case. 'You make good music,' she said. 'I could learn. You could teach me. I learn music fast. And I could dance, rock and roll. We could do an act together.'

And someone who made films for TV might be using the Métro, she thought, someone whose eyes you could see, someone who was looking for something special, not just a girl riding on a carousel. And a double act would be safer than going solo. The someone would watch and listen and then take out that important piece of paper... but first, she remembered, she'd have to learn to write her name.

'What about your gran?' Paul was saying.

'What about her?' shouted Rose. 'This won't do, you know. I've got my eye on you, young man,' she said accusingly.' She's too young for you, a kid. You won't get away with it, you know...'

'Oh, Rose,' said Maritsa, blushing. 'I didn't mean that!'

'They say you're all musicians,' mused Paul. 'Naturals. Like breathing.'

'The *dad* plays fiddle.' Maritsa pulled a face. 'And my brothers play mouth organ. It sounds awful!'

'Ah,' said Paul sharply. 'The brothers.'

'Two ugly brothers,' Maritsa said quickly.

'Do they beat you, too?' asked Paul.

'Those two?' Maritsa laughed. 'They're just kids.'

'I like kids.' Paul frowned. 'Heard a kid went missing the other day. She'd been sleeping rough, like you. I've got a kid sister. Nine. Makes you think, doesn't it?'

Then he had a home, a family.

'Where do you sleep?' she asked him.

'Here and there.' Paul grinned. 'A bit like you lot.'

'You can't be like us,' said Maritsa scornfully. 'Because you're just a *gadjé*. But you still make good music,' she conceded.

Paul seemed to notice the cake boxes for the first time. 'What do you keep in there?'

Maritsa opened them up. The remaining cakes were fast becoming a sticky mess.

'Want one?'

Paul shook his head. 'I must be off now,' he said. 'But I'll give you a hand first. With the old lady,' he added softly, but Rose had heard.

'I can manage,' she protested loudly. 'I was riding around on the Métro before you were even thought of, young man.'

Paul walked with them as far as the ticket barrier. 'Hopping in and out of the Métro,' he said. 'Must cost you a fortune...'

Maritsa was surprised. He was a busker, he should know. 'The mama buys us weekly tickets.'

'Then there is a mama?'

Maritsa stiffened. 'Not *my* mama.'

'So where is your mama?'

'I told you, she's dead,' said Maritsa. 'And that's true.'

'And your dad? He dead, too?'

'Oh, he's busy,' Maritsa said airily.

'My son,' announced Rose unexpectedly, 'is a very impor-tant man. Works on TV.'

Paul frowned. He looked from Maritsa to Rose and back to Maritsa. 'Then you really are...'

But Maritsa was triumphant.

'Didn't I *tell* you?' she crowed. 'She's my *gran!*'

CHAPTER EIGHT

Along one of the passageways, four Arab drummers had set up camp, squatting on the ground, lost in their music. A little crowd had gathered to listen. People threw coins but the musicians didn't seem to notice. They weren't playing for an audience, they were playing for themselves.

Entranced, as always, by the sound, Maritsa lingered. Rose tugged at her arm. 'Arabs,' she warned. 'A bunch of rogues, conmen...' But still Maritsa didn't move. 'Please yourself, *mademoiselle*,' sniffed Rose at last and she shuffled away.

The musicians took a break. Their faces lost their rapt expressions. Suddenly they were just a group of sweaty, dark-haired men sitting in a circle. One of them lit up the stub of a cigarette. People drifted away. The magic had fizzled out.

Tentatively Maritsa put out a finger and touched the leather tassel on one of the drums. Its owner looked up at her and grinned. He ran his hand over the drumskin and beat out a soft staccato. One of the others began picking out a slow, insistent rhythm. The first man replied at a slightly higher pitch.

The smoking man stubbed out his cigarette, grinding it into the floor with brown-stained fingers and added a third strand. The fourth musician frowned, listened, waited for the right moment, smiled and started to play. Now all four drums were playing. Maritsa arranged herself on the floor. She longed to join in. It looked so easy. Nothing to it. One day she'd buy herself a little drum...

It was late when the musicians decided, without uttering a single word, to pack it in. When Maritsa got up she was stiff and aching. She stumbled along to the platform. Rose was curled up, asleep. Maritsa sighed. There was no room beside her; she'd taken up all three seats. Maritsa tried to stretch out against the wall but the ground was hard and lumpy. She wondered where the homeless family slept; she hadn't noticed them when they'd come back from the snack bar. Oh, for a soft bed, thought Maritsa longingly.

But that little blonde show-off didn't deserve a bed.

The last trains came and went. The man in uniform came down the platform. A woman came with him. She was carrying a Thermos flask.

'Some hot soup for Bertrand's old lady,' she said.

The man frowned at Maritsa. 'Station's closed,' he said, seizing her by the arm. 'I'll see you off.'

Maritsa pointed at Rose. 'I'm with her.'

'Gypsy liar. You came last night, you know you did. And

you'll leave tonight, if I have anything to do with it. Don't your people have a caravan? An authorized campsite?'

'If she can stay,' said Maritsa stubbornly, 'why can't I?'

'I'll throw her out too, one of these fine days.'

'I would like to see you try!' Rose was sitting up, looking fierce. She pointed a finger at the man in uniform. 'You were always a problem child, Bertrand Leblanc.'

Bertrand looked embarrassed. 'I let you stay, Rose...'

Rose corrected him. '*Mademoiselle* to you, *if* you please.'

'...because you're old and you've got nowhere to go and because you were once my teacher. I shouldn't do it. It's against the rules. I could lose my job tomorrow over you and I've got too many mouths to feed.' His voice was pleading now. 'But that girl's a gypsy. She's got a home to go to. Better off than us, most of them are...'

'Rubbish,' said Rose. 'That girl is my grandchild. If she goes, I go too. And you can take your nasty soup away,' she added. 'We've already eaten.' She looked coy. 'With a *gentleman*.'

'Who's telling lies now?' challenged Maritsa after he'd gone. 'You're not really my grannie. You know that.'

'I never tell lies,' said Rose. 'And I do have a son.'

'Then why doesn't he take care of you?'

'He would have,' said Rose vaguely, 'if he could.' She looked hard at Maritsa. 'He's a professor, your papa,' she said. 'At the Sorbonne.'

'I don't want him to be a professor,' Maritsa said. 'That's boring. You said he made films. Big American films, for TV.'

'No I didn't,' said Rose.

Maritsa was irritated. 'You don't know my dad.'

Rose adjusted her hat. 'Do you?'

'My dad's a prince,' said Maritsa desperately.

'A professor would be easier,' Rose pointed out. 'My own papa's a professor...'

Maritsa thought about Rose's papa. 'He must be billions of years old,' she said. 'He must be dead.' But Rose was already settling down, plucking at her blanket, fiddling with her coat.

Maritsa cuddled up to her, fitting herself around the fat, cushiony shape. Rose smelt awful, she thought. Who wanted a grannie who smelt like that? Then she sighed. The old woman was hopeless; even as a prop she was hopeless and anyway, Maritsa was sick of sleeping rough.

But a star... me, a star, she remembered and she drifted into visions of glitter and lights, of rainbow leggings and sequined tops, gold hoop earrings and bangles and glass shoes with diamond buckles and delicate high heels. Yet somewhere just outside the glitter lurked the eyeless man with his fat pink lips and his foxy moustache, perpetually sucking his caramel creams, a dodgy man, a man you couldn't trust. But he was podgy, he was old and she was tough, strong, streetwise – she could easily take care of him. And he was only the beginning. She could just use him to get started. There'd be plenty of others, once she was known...

She woke up aching, rearranged herself, drowsed, wriggled, woke again, transferred herself to the floor and slept heavily. The first train of the morning charged in like a roaring tiger, a wild forest beast she had to fight off. She forced open her sting-ing eyes. Above her the old woman lay snoring.

A gnawing hunger pushed the confusion of dreams away. Money? She had enough. She shook out her skirts, finger-combed her hair and rebraided her plaits, expertly weaving into them the shiny cake box ribbons.

Upstairs the snack bar was just opening. Outside, croissants lay warm and fragrant on their big wooden tray. The woman came out and hauled it inside, scowling at Maritsa. 'Not you again.'

When she got back to the platform, Rose was beginning to stir.

'Brought you some breakfast.'

Rose looked at her blankly.

'Food,' snapped Maritsa. 'Something to eat. Bread.'

Rose sat up. She took the offered sandwich and examined it suspiciously, removing the top crust and sniffing at the piece of ham and the chopped lettuce leaves. Then she picked them off delicately, put them in her mouth and began to chew them laboriously, like an ancient goat.

Maritsa had had enough. She was tired and aching and fed up with this smelly, ungrateful old bag. A train was approaching. She could get away. Instantly. Cleanly. No looking back. No goodbyes.

The doors slid open and she hopped on board, but the train just sat there, not moving, running to time.

The signal changed and the carriage doors jammed on Rose's slow-moving bulk.

Maritsa's heart sank.

'I'm working by myself today, *Grand-mère*,' she said coldly.

The automatic doors slid back and released the old woman. Rose turned and glared at them. 'I should think so too,' she said, stepping inside with great dignity and arranging herself fussily next to Maritsa. As the train moved out, she leaned across and tapped the silky knees of the woman opposite. 'Those doors are dangerous,' she announced loudly. 'Don't you agree, *madame*?'

But the woman swung sideways and frowned at her magazine.

Rose looked miffed. 'I said those doors are dangerous. Are you deaf, *madame*?'

Maritsa was horrified. She was worse than the boys.

'I shall write a letter of complaint,' shouted Rose. 'To the management.'

'Oh, shut up, *Grand-mère!*' hissed Maritsa.

But Rose turned on her. 'I'm not your gran.'

Maritsa had had enough. She took herself off to the end of the carriage. No point in begging now, she thought. No point in trying to work through this lot, with that old hag down there blowing her top.

Suddenly the door between the carriages was banged open, a mouth organ trilled unmusically and a crumpled note was thrust under her nose, with a giggle.

'Give us a couple of francs, *mademoiselle...*'

Maritsa recognized their voices before she saw them, but because they no longer seemed to have anything much to do with her she didn't try to escape.

'So look who's here!' The boy spoke in Rom.

'Sister Maritsa!'

She sat, unable to move.

'Where've you been?'

'What have you been doing?'

She said nothing.

'Just wait till you get home. Just wait.'

'I'm not going home,' said Maritsa defiantly.

'What do you mean?'

'Where are you going to sleep? Where've you been sleeping?'

Nikolas sniggered. 'Who've you been sleeping with? Some *gadjo* boy?'

'A tart,' sniggered Stefan. 'Like her mama.'

Maritsa cheeks burned and she slapped him.

'Sorry,' sang Stefan. 'Didn't mean it, didn't mean it...'

'Come on, Maritsa.' Nikolas's voice was plaintive now. 'You've got us into enough trouble. And the mama's worried sick...'

That made Maritsa feel bad.

The train slid slowly into a station.

The mama had always been good to her, thought Maritsa. The poor mama. She really ought to go back.

But as the doors opened, Stefan lunged forward, grabbed her arm, pinching the flesh so it hurt and started dragging her towards the open door.

Never mind the mama, thought Maritsa. 'I'm not coming!' she shouted, struggling. 'I won't!'

'Leave that girl alone.'

Caught by surprise, Stefan let go. Then he saw the old woman. 'Shut your face, you old *khan*,' he said weakly.

'Get off this train,' ordered Rose and to the boys' own surprise, they did.

'Who's she?' yelped Stefan through the closing doors.

'My gran,' yelled Maritsa.

'You haven't got a gran,' she saw him mouth through the window.

Rose subsided on to a seat. 'Young hooligans,' she muttered. 'Ought to be at school.'

But Maritsa was confused. 'They were my brothers,' she said. 'But not my real brothers...' It was puzzling; Rose had rescued her again. 'Where do you think you're going, *Grand-mère?*' she asked at last.

Rose gave a wide, gap-toothed grin. 'Going for a ride,' she said smugly.

The train stopped at the next station and the doors slid open. Rose heaved herself upright and clambered out. Baffled, Maritsa followed her.

'Where are you off to now?'

Rose turned and nodded. 'I've enjoyed my ride, thank you, *mademoiselle,*' she said politely. 'Now I must go home.' She shuffled slowly around to the opposite platform. She had obviously made the round trip many times before.

On the train back to St Michel, Rose slumped into sleep. She looked grey; she looked dead.

Maritsa slipped off her grand shoes and tucked them behind her. 'My grannie is sick,' she said, holding out her hand.

But Rose opened her eyes. 'No, I'm not,' she said.

Back at St Michel, they walked slowly along the connecting passageway.

'Do you always come back to the same place?' asked Maritsa.

'Of course...' Rose looked at her sharply. 'I'm not like you lot, never satisfied with one place, always on the move. Besides, there's Bertrand...' She paused. 'I'm stopping here,' she announced.

She arranged herself comfortably on the ground, her bulging bags drawn in close and her back against the curve of the tiled wall.

Maritsa hung around for a while, not knowing what else to do. She considered writing the message: MY GRAN IS OLD AND SICK... but Rose would probably mess things up again.

She spotted the rolled-up magazine in one of Rose's bags.

'Teach me some hard words,' she said, pulling it out.

But Rose was singing. '*I regret nothing,*' she warbled in an out-of-tune treble, '*no, nothing at all...* That's an old Piaf song,' she boasted.

Someone laughed and threw down a couple of coins.

Maritsa was bored. Between them, she thought, they could have made a fortune, but Rose had to do it her way.

It really was time to give up, go home. She'd never make

enough for that little room and she was sick of sleeping rough; she felt dirty and she ached; she'd stayed too long in one place and it was time to move on. And back there was the mama being worried sick; what was a fake *grand-mère* compared with that? The fosterchild gone missing...

They'd have sent out seekers by now, she supposed, but there wouldn't be any clues: Maritsa's *patrins* could have been anyone's *patrins.* And kids *did* go missing in the Métro. That man Paul thought she didn't know, but she did. There was that little kid who'd got cut off from her group by the rush-hour mob. They'd spent weeks searching, but she never turned up. Her mama still sobbed and wailed, but she never told, never called the cops. What was the point? One gypsy less? The cops would be delighted.

She thought about the mama being worried sick.

Or had those boys been lying? After all, she was one mouth less to feed...

The boys, she thought. Her stepbrothers, her two ugly stepbrothers. Who wanted to go back to those little horrors? Yet they could sometimes be kind, they could often, even, be fun.

She remembered the pilgrimage to Saintes Maries-de-la-Mer, when the three of them had run hand in hand, dancing, splashing each other, following the procession of gilded shrines into the candlelit sea. But they'd been younger then and so had she. She'd made a wish there, she remembered, dutifully laying one of her scarves at the feet of St Sarah-la-Kali and asking for the mama, when she was of age, to find her a good man. This year her request would be different; there were other things she wanted now.

Her empty stomach distracted her. How much money was left? She checked secretly. Just enough.

Abandoning Rose in mid-performance, she walked along to the escalators and found the homeless woman's daughter hassling people as they stepped off and Marcel huddled, knees up, absorbed in some secret game.

The girl spotted her. 'You still reading *Cinderella*, gypsy?'

'I read all of your magazine,' sniffed Maritsa, 'but my gran says it's rubbish.'

The girl looked incredulous. 'Your *gran*?' she sneered. 'What, that batty old thing?' She made a lunge at Marcel. 'You're dripping again,' she said, wiping his nose with a rag. She hauled him upright. Marcel struggled and fought, but his sister won. 'You've got a cold, lovey,' she said, suddenly maternal. 'It's all this bad air...' She yelled across at their mother, 'I'm taking him outside!'

CHAPTER NINE

Maritsa rode up behind them.

'There's a big park out there,' said the girl, looking down at her. 'Did you know that, gypsy? I'm taking the kid. Come with us if you like.'

Maritsa followed them on to the concourse. She glanced at the snack bar but remembered pancakes.

The girl looked back at her. 'There's a carousel, too,' she said. 'We saw it. Yesterday.' She ruffled Marcel's hair. 'Want to go on the horsies again?'

Maritsa hung around the concourse for a bit, then followed them out. That day there was no sun and the sky was ashen and chill. Even at noon, the shops and bistros had switched on their outside lights.

Along the boulevard, she found Marcel wandering aimlessly, while his sister drooled over window displays. Maritsa tried to take his hand but he snatched it away. 'Gypsy,' he spat.

She caught up with the girl. Marcel tagged along behind.

'See that jacket?' The girl pointed. 'I'm having that.'

'Well you can't,' argued Maritsa. 'Because I saw it first.'

The girl was indignant. 'I picked it out yesterday.'

'Well, I chose it first,' said Maritsa, sticking out her tongue.

The girl pulled a face. 'You're disgusting,' she said. 'A proper gypsy.' She nudged Marcel. 'Look at her — a real gypsy.'

'Well you're just a *gadji*,' retorted Maritsa. 'And *gadja* don't count.'

'*I'm* not a gadget,' protested Marcel.

'Yes you are,' snapped the girl. 'The gypsy said you are, so you are one.'

Marcel scowled at Maritsa. 'Don't like gypsies,' he said.

They crossed the road and went into the park.

'Pancakes,' said Maritsa.

The girl sniffed. 'Don't get the idea I'm treating you.'

Ahead of them, the scent of warm vanilla rose from the green-painted pancake stall and, brilliant against the sombre foliage, the little carousel was twinkling and spinning like a witch ball.

They joined a small queue. Marcel stood apart, already enchanted by the fairy lights and painted horses. His sister wiped his nose brutally.

'Ow!' he complained. Then he pointed. 'Want a ride on one of those horsies.'

'Well, you'll just have to wait.' The girl ordered two pancakes.

The pancake man suddenly spotted Maritsa. 'Ah! The rich

gypsy with the fancy shoes,' he said, winking. 'Thought they'd locked you up.'

'No one locks me up,' said Maritsa sharply. 'And there are plenty of other pancake stalls.'

'OK, OK.' The man ladled a thin coat of batter on to the griddle. 'What's your fancy today, rich *mademoiselle*? Jam? Chestnut? Champagne?'

The two girls found a bench and sat down.

'Where did you get them fancy shoes?'

'Found them,' said Maritsa.

'Bet you nicked them,' said the girl.

'Think what you like, *gadji*...' Maritsa noticed with pleasure a streak of melted jam across the front of the girl's blue jumper. She was so clean, so brushed, so neat. She couldn't possibly, realized Maritsa, have spent the night in the Métro.

'Where do you sleep?' she asked.

'At our gran's,' said the girl.

It was all an act, then. They weren't homeless. All lies.

'She's got a place,' the girl went on. She jerked a finger at Marcel. 'The kid sleeps with Mum.' She sighed. 'My grannie snores,' she said, 'and she kicks me in the night.' She stared at Maritsa. 'You sleep with your gran?'

Maritsa nodded.

'She got a place?'

'Not yet,' said Maritsa.

The girl pulled a face. 'She sleeps down there? No wonder she's smelly...' She suddenly thought of something. 'She looks too old to be your gran. Is she really your gran?'

'Oh yes,' said Maritsa. 'And my dad's a —' she remembered — 'professor. What does your dad do?'

'My dad's a bastard,' said the girl briefly.

The carousel stopped. They walked Marcel over. The girl lifted him on to a horse and pushed a five-franc coin into his hand. 'You give that to the nice man,' she told him. 'Like yesterday.'

The music started. The horse lifted. Marcel slid his arms around its painted neck and the coin fell out. It rolled across the boards and dropped at Maritsa's feet. She picked it up and offered it to the showman. 'It's for that little boy.' She pointed.

The showman gave her a hard look. 'So where's your fancy man today, gypsy?'

'What's he mean?' asked the girl.

'Nothing.' Maritsa blushed angrily. 'He's just stupid, that's all.'

They stood watching the horses turning, waving dutifully at Marcel each time he came round.

'You know, I *will* get that jacket before you,' the girl said dreamily. 'I'll really get it.'

'How? Are you going to steal it?'

'We don't steal things. Not like you lot.' The girl moved in close. 'Can you keep a secret?'

'What secret?' asked Maritsa.

'I'm going to make pots of money. Buy my mum somewhere nice to live, a proper room for Marcel...'

'M-m-m,' said Maritsa, unimpressed. It was too close to her own dreams, of that little room, of that songbird in a cage.

'I know you don't believe me but it's true.' The girl preened herself, running her fingers through her fine blonde hair.

The carousel slowed and stopped. Marcel began to slither down.

'Want another ride?' offered his sister.

Marcel looked astonished. Then he nodded and grinned.

The girl handed a coin to the showman. 'The kid always drops it,' she explained.

The music started. Marcel caressed the horse's ears.

'Can you keep another secret?'

Maritsa nodded generously. Who cared about this girl's silly secrets? And anyway, who was there to tell?

'I've got a boyfriend,' whispered the girl. 'My mum doesn't know. I'm meeting him today. Round the back of the park. He asked Marcel to come, too, but since you're here...' She was already edging away.

'Hey!' protested Maritsa, but she was caught, she was trapped. 'Hey!' she yelled. 'That's not fair.' But the girl had vanished into the shadows.

Maritsa followed her down the path. From somewhere ahead, a figure turned, paused. 'Wait there for me!' the girl called. 'I won't be long. If the kid gets fed up, take him back down to our mum.' Then she darted into the bushes and disappeared.

Maritsa was furious. She didn't want to be stuck with that snivelling brat. It was the same with the *kumpania*; why did they always dump their toddlers on to her? She'd even looked after the boys when they were small, wiped their snotty little noses and never a thank-you...

She walked back along the path, then turned up towards the lake. The kid would be all right, she thought. The girl would be back soon. She had to be. She wouldn't leave her little brother for long in the care of a gypsy. For Maritsa knew the stories the *gadjé* invented – how gypsies kidnapped *gadjé* children (as if they didn't have enough kids of their own).

She found the steps again and ran up them, pausing between the two stone ladies to look down at the lake. Above her, in the sullen sky, a heron was hovering, dark against the dirty clouds. It dived suddenly, spreading its wings wide and, landing on the edge of the silvery green water, retracted itself into a motionless black squiggle.

Maritsa shivered. She knew the legends from home, how the restless dead could come back in other forms and prey on the living, suck out their blood. A heron was harmless.

But was it just a heron?

She stood watching it, black and immobile on its stone, one leg raised, not moving, not a flutter, not a twitch, unreal. How could a real bird stay like that? She watched it, half-expecting it to rise up in the shape of a giant bat, a vampire. Evil could take many forms, she thought. People back home said that a vampire could pass for a really dishy male in a black swirling cape, but never (she grinned, remembering) a fat bloke with a taste for caramel creams.

Wilhelm, she thought. Not a nice man, but no vampire...

Just a film director. *If* he hadn't lied.

She could walk round to his Café Lauré and find out. Call his bluff; after all, he'd invited her. 'So show me your movie cameras,' she could challenge him. And if it was true and she was good enough (and she *knew* she was good enough), then he'd have to cough up. Maritsa knew the form. She'd seen it in a film on TV. There'd be a lawyer's paper with her name printed on it. Then money. Lots of money. But she'd still have to learn how to sign her name...

Famous people, pop stars like the ones in Sylvie's magazine, had to start somewhere, she knew that. Maybe they just put up with people like Wilhelm.

But suppose he were a fake? Up to no good? An odd, evil man who'd kidnap her?

Things happened. Things talked about in whispers, glossed over, hushed up, but Maritsa was no fool. Things happened. To kids, even. That busker Paul knew.

And the little brat was out there in the dusk, all by himself...

Maritsa ran back — there seemed to be nothing else to do — and found Marcel sitting folornly on a bench.

'I've come back for you,' she said virtuously.

Marcel drew back and began to whimper.

'Oh, shut up,' said Maritsa. 'Sylvie hasn't gone for good. She went to see a friend, that's all.' She stared back along the paths, trying to pierce through the shadows. Why? she thought; why? Why take the kid out and then leave him? He could have stayed behind with their mum.

'I'm cold,' cried Marcel.

Maritsa zipped up his threadbare anorak and pulled up the hood. 'She'll be back soon,' she said. 'You'll see...' *And I'll be so mad with her,* she added silently, *that I'll probably hit her!* She took out some money. 'Want to go on the horses again?'

But Marcel shook his head. 'Want Sylvie,' he pouted.

'Don't want you. You're a gypsy.'

Maritsa suddenly remembered what the girl had told her —
take the kid home if he gets fed up.

'Want to go home?' she said. 'Back to your mum?'

Marcel wiped his nose on the back of his hand.

'Not going with you.'

'Then we'll just have to wait here,' said Maritsa brightly.
'She won't be much longer.'

They sat. They waited.

Marcel brought out his collection of used tickets and
played games on the bench.

It grew darker.

By half-past three the pancake man was packing up, pad-
locking the stall with a big iron key. He glanced across at them.

'Ought to take that kid home,' he said. 'Catch his death in
this weather...' He paused, trying to work things out. 'That
other girl his sister?'

Maritsa nodded. 'We're waiting for her.'

'Well, you can't wait much longer...' The man looked at his
watch. 'They'll be shutting the place up at four...' He grimaced
at Marcel. 'Lock you in,' he joked. 'Then what would you do?'

The music from the carousel wound down and stopped.
The last customers were lifted off and swept away by grown-

ups. The showman checked on his day's takings. Then he switched off the fairy lights.

Marcel watched them go out.

'Want a horsy ride,' he whined.

'Well, you can't now,' said Maritsa. 'He's switched it all off.'

'Want Sylvie...'

Maritsa took a deep breath.

'Let's go and look for her, shall we?' At least, she thought, it would keep them both warm.

She grabbed his hand. This time he didn't protest.

They ran along the path, calling her: 'Sylvie! Sylvie!'

They walked round the outer edge of the park and out through the gates on the other side. They looked up and down the street and across the road, but there was no small blonde girl in a nice blue jumper and tattered jeans.

They went back to the park and walked round the lake. A light breeze was curling the water into little shiny folds and dry leaves scuttered along the gravel paths like skeletal spiders. Maritsa checked. The heron had gone.

'I'm cold,' complained Marcel.

'So am I,' sighed Maritsa. 'So is everybody.'

They heard an insistent ringing sound and at the top of the steps they found a man with a handbell.

'Closing time,' he called.

'I'll take you home,' said Maritsa. 'Come on, let's run.' But where had the heron gone? she wondered uneasily. Had it turned into a bat, a vampire? Might it be lurking in the shadows, ready to swoop, to pounce, to sink its needle teeth into her throat? People she could manage, Maritsa wasn't scared of people, but spirits that fluttered inside darkness, the faceless things that could lurk inside night shadows, those were something else.

She tried to hide her fear from Marcel.

'Let's be horsies,' she urged to keep him going, 'galloping through the night.' But Marcel was such a *little* foal and, 'Closing time!' the men were shouting, rattling their keys.

'Sylvie!' gasped Marcel.

Maritsa crouched. 'Climb up on my back,' she said. 'I'll be your horsy...'

She staggered across the Boulevard St Michel. That little brat weighed a ton, but anger gave her strength.

Anger and indignation. When she caught up with Marcel's big sister, she'd give her a piece of her mind. How could she abandon a little kid like that?

The mama... worried sick, nagged an unwelcome voice inside her head. Yes, but that's different, thought Maritsa. And I didn't really abandon the boys – those two brats knew how to take care of themselves. Stefan's eight, Nikolas is nine, this one's just a baby. Three? Four?

She dumped him at the top of the Métro steps.

'You can do the rest by yourself,' she said. 'You're heavy.'

Marcel looked at her and his face crumpled.

'Want Sylvie...'

'Well, I haven't got her,' Maritsa snapped.

At the bottom of the escalators, Sylvie's mum was sitting in her usual place, passive, propped against the tiles, her HOME-LESS placard dangling from her neck. Her blank eyes lit up at the sight of Marcel.

'Where's your sister?' she asked.

'She went off,' said Maritsa.

Marcel, cuddled close to the woman, looked suddenly baleful. 'That gypsy turned Sylvie into a gadget,' he accused.

The woman passed an exhausted hand over her forehead. 'Where is she, gypsy?'

'Don't know.'

'You must know,' said the woman. 'She must have told you where she was going...'

'A friend,' said Marcel. 'Sylvie went to see a friend.'

'What friend?' asked the woman. 'Where?'

But secrets were always sacred, even *gadjé* secrets and Maritsa wouldn't tell. Tell a secret and your tongue shrivelled. Betray someone and you'd be sure to die.

She suddenly remembered Rose. 'Got to go to my gran.'

'So have we,' the woman shouted after her. 'And if Sylvie doesn't turn up, what'll we do?'

Maritsa really didn't care. It was none of her business. Rose was none of her business either, she thought. It was time to give up on this crazy game. Time to go home.

On the platform she found Rose sitting upright on the yellow plastic seats, drinking wine out of a paper cup, prissily blotting her mouth with a tissue. Across her lap lay the messy remains of a sandwich.

Maritsa felt unexpectedly jealous.

'Who bought you all that stuff?'

'Aah!' said Rose coyly. 'Wouldn't you like to know?'

'I've been in the park,' said Maritsa. 'With that blonde girl and her brother.' A train came thundering in and she paused while people jostled past them. The doors slid shut and it began to move out. 'That girl ran away and left me with the kid.' Rose didn't seem to be listening. 'I brought him back to his mama. I think that girl's really run away,' she added loudly, exaggerating in order to get some response.

Rose blinked. 'Girls who run away,' she declared, 'always come to a bad end.'

'Well, I've run away,' said Maritsa, 'and I'm all right.'

'Oh, but that's different,' declared Rose. 'You've got me.'

CHAPTER TEN

Maritsa felt irritated.

Was that how the old woman saw things?

Well, her grandchild had been lying – she *wasn't* all right. She was tired and she ached and she'd wasted most of a day and made no money. And if that girl Sylvie didn't turn up, it was she who'd get the blame. The dream had turned sour. It really *was* time to go home. And Rose wasn't making that easy.

So Maritsa reminded herself of those three moulded seats, whose curved ridges, designed to enclose three bottoms, had last night bitten into her ribcage, stomach and thighs. And she looked down at the hard concrete floor and thought of her own soft bed on the travellers' site. Suddenly, putting up with the boys seemed a small price to pay.

And they weren't really bad. They just liked showing off. There were even a few times, she remembered, when she'd almost been fond of them.

But she couldn't turn up empty-handed. The mama would be angry enough as it was.

She made up her mind. That evening, she would work for a bit. Then, when she'd made a decent amount, she'd get on the line for Gennevilliers.

It was time to move on.

She pulled a discarded plastic carrier from a refuse bin and reached for her book, which was sticking out of one of Rose's bags. And as soon as the next train came thundering in, she gave the old woman a butterfly kiss on each cheek. 'Bye, *Grand-mère!*'

She leapt on board just as the doors began to close. 'I'm going home,' she shouted. 'But I'll come back and see you...' The heavy glass cut off her words.

Pushing away the image of Rose's puzzled face, Maritsa slipped off her shoes and dropped them into the bag. She wiggled her toes, quite pleased to be barefoot again. Those shoes didn't seem quite so desirable now. The uppers were scuffed, the heels were chipped and they'd left red, sore places all over her feet. *Grand-mère* had been right, she thought. They *were* silly. But, oh, if only she had lots of pairs, rows and rows of beautiful silly shoes, it wouldn't matter if they wore out and didn't fit. She could wear a different pair every day and they'd fit in different places so her feet would never get rubbed...

She stopped herself dreaming.

She had work to do.

She took out the note, grimy, creased, but still readable. Then she walked along the carriages, waiting politely for the few who were prepared to read it, to notice the nakedness of

her feet in mid-December and she said her *'pleases'* so pleading-
ly and her *'thank yous'* so gratefully that after half a dozen carriages she'd done rather well.

She sat down, feeling pleased with herself. Soon the warmth
of the carriage and the soothing rhythm of the train began
making her drowsy, so she closed her eyes and let herself drift,
enjoying the smooth, unlumpy comfort of the seat.

Doors slid open and closed, opened and closed.

Grand-mère... thought Maritsa.

Somebody stumbled over her feet. 'Pardon, *mademoiselle.'*

I could take Rose back with me, Maritsa told herself; someone would find her a bed. But would an old *gadji* live with gypsies? But if she learned some Rom she might start a little
school: she'd enjoy that. The social workers had already suggested a visiting teacher for the kids, but who wanted some *gadjo*
to tell you what to do?

But Rose was different. Rose was *family.*

'This is my Granddaughter,' she'd say in that posh voice she
sometimes put on and the kids wouldn't dare argue. No. They'd
be impressed.

'And she knows who my dad is,' Maritsa could hear herself
boasting to the boys. 'My dad's a professor!'

'Don't be stupid!' Nikolas sniped. 'Anyway, you're dreaming.
You're asleep... The girl's asleep.' His voice had changed, was

much older, slightly accented. 'Nice little piece, what do you think?'

Maritsa jerked up her head and stared with shocked fascination at the liverish moustache and the black mirrored shades.

'The gypsy and I are old friends,' Wilhelm was explaining to the woman beside him. 'I buy her cakes. Now don't be jealous, *chérie*,' he added playfully. He cupped his hand over Maritsa's knee. 'Meet my lady wife...' The blonde woman interrupted her chewing with the briefest of smiles. 'She's in the film business too – aren't you, Chloe?'

Maritsa felt confused. His *wife*? That made things OK. Yet he still felt wrong.

Perhaps she wasn't his wife. Maybe he was lying.

The woman came over and sat beside her. 'Hello dear. Like a lollipop?' Maritsa gratefully unwrapped a Raspberry Fizz. 'Wilhelm's been telling me all about you,' she confided. 'You should see the photos he took...' Her perfume enveloped Maritsa, making her sneeze. 'Bless you!' said the woman. 'Are you catching a cold? You know,' she whispered confidentially, 'we use a lot of kids like you. And there's lots of money in it. No more bare feet...' She shook her head over Maritsa's grubby toes. 'Have you seen this poor kid's feet, Wilhelm?'

'She's got shoes,' said Wilhelm shortly. 'She pinched them.'

Maritsa drew back, shocked. Someone might have heard him.

Below the reddish moustache, the pink lips pursed in fake disapproval, then parted in a triumphant grin. 'Caught you again, didn't I?' He paused. 'Let's have a look at your bit of paper.' He reached over and took it. *Father dead. Mother ill,* he read aloud, with a stage sigh. 'Oh dear, very sad, very sad.' He handed it back with two fifty-franc notes. 'Go to the market tomorrow,' he said. 'Rue de Cherche Midi — they should have some bargain trainers.'

Maritsa stared at him, curling her fingers tightly around the notes. This bloke handed out money like a bag of cheap sweets...

The train slowed and the couple got up.

The woman adjusted her long silky coat. 'We're always on the lookout for fresh talent, dear. That's why we noticed you.' Maritsa admired her silver leather boots with the shiny black buttons. 'I know — why don't you come back with us right now? We could give you a screen test tonight.'

Maritsa hesitated. This might be her big chance. Money, she thought. She could go home later, load the mama and the boys with presents, buy some liquor for her stepdad, maybe even get Rose a new hat. And she saw glittery dresses and diamond earrings and rows and rows of silly shoes and lace curtains patterned with cherubs and hearts in her own little room with the songbird in a cage...

But she still couldn't see the man's eyes.

Maritsa sucked on the lollipop. She needed to talk to some-one, but who was there to ask? What did Rose know of the world? And if she went home, the boys would tease her: Maritsa? A star? And the mama would laugh. And the others would say: a real gypsy doesn't need that kind of money, a gypsy doesn't need a little room that never moves, a gypsy has the sky and the open road. It's your *gadjé* blood that makes you hanker after things like that...

'We'd run you back afterwards.'

'It's not safe,' said the woman, 'for a young girl like you, on the Métro late at night. Anything could happen.'

She seems nice, thought Maritsa. Caring. The mama might have said something like that.

She played for time. 'I'd have to ask my gran first...'

'Is that where you sleep?' asked Wilhelm. He sounded vaguely disappointed. 'I thought you told me you slept in the Métro.'

'Oh no,' protested Maritsa. 'I stay with my gran at night. My gran's got a little room.'

'Not a caravan?' said Wilhelm. 'A trailer? She's a gypsy, isn't she? I thought she'd sleep in a caravan.'

'Then you thought wrong,' Maritsa snapped.

The doors slid open and the couple got out.

'Come and see us at the Café Laure,' called the woman, 'if you change your mind. But you'll have to make it snappy – we won't be there for much longer. And there's no shortage of girls who want to make it to the top.'

I might even do that, thought Maritsa. Hang around for one more day, maybe two. Go out with them for a screen test and after that, who could say?

And she couldn't really leave her *grand-mère*. Not coldly, like that: *'Goodbye Gran, I'm going home.'* It wasn't on. It wasn't fair.

And anyway she needed to give that kid Sylvie a hard time. Just wait till she showed up tomorrow morning!

She changed at Denfert-Rochereau and spent the next hour or so playing the trains, working out her routes from the coloured lines on the maps. By the time she got back to St Michel she was hungry all over again.

But before she looked for something to eat, she thought she'd cross over and check on Rose.

Along the passageway she found herself following a yellow canvas bag with pink and orange letters. She was amusing her-self by stringing the letters together inside her head when the bag was set down, then opened with a flourish by the woman who was carrying it.

'Ladies and gentlemen,' the woman announced, drawing

herself back against the wall, 'The Magic Métro Company proudly presents CINDERELLA.'

'I've got that story!' cried Maritsa delightedly. She took the book out of her bag and held it up. 'See?'

The woman looked pleased. 'You'll enjoy it then.'

The two men who were with her unrolled a screen of red and blue stripes sewn with little bells and sequins. A crowd began to gather – people who'd been working late in shops and offices, children who'd been taken out for Christmas treats.

The woman stood behind the screen and smiled as if she were on stage, her long brown hair cascading from a small embroidered cap.

Down behind the screen the men had been busy and now, over the top, appeared Cinderella in rags, followed by a ginger fur cat. Maritsa clapped loudly.

'S-s-s-sh,' people said, but Maritsa didn't care.

The ugly sisters appeared, with noses of crimson satin and wigs of curled wool. And the story unfolded.

Cinderella sighed. 'Oh, I *do* want to go to the prince's ball...'

'Then you shall,' promised a fairy with bright, gauzy wings. 'Just close your eyes.'

Maritsa closed hers and waited. What a splendid act it was, she thought. What a fun way to make money! If she didn't pass the screen test she could do this instead.

'If you think the world is bad,' the fairy was saying, 'then make up another one. And remember – if you want to be a princess, you can be a princess!' And when Maritsa opened her eyes, she saw a prince in purple satin and Cinderella all sparkly in a spangled white dress.

And Maritsa herself danced at the prince's ball, her flowered skirts swaying over her silly, pretty shoes and the prince had Paul's face – his nice pussycat eyes and his reddish-brown stubble...

All too soon it was over, the striped cloth rolled up, the puppets replaced inside the yellow canvas bag. The crowd dispersed, but Maritsa hung around.

'I want to ask you something,' she said to the woman, pushing one of Wilhelm's fifty-franc notes into the collecting box.

The woman looked interested. 'Go ahead,' she said.

'I liked your story. I liked your puppets.'

'Thank you,' said the woman. 'That's nice.'

Maritsa took a deep breath. 'I want to join your Magic Métro Company.'

The woman smiled gently. 'We don't make a fortune, you know,' she said. 'You'd do better by yourself. Do you know anything about puppets?'

Maritsa shook her head. 'But I could learn,' she said. 'I learn fast. I'm learning to read,' she added proudly. 'My gran's teaching me.' Rose could help, she thought. She could find them new stories.

'We'd love to have you,' said one of the men, 'but we can't. Three people is right, four would be too many. And besides, don't you have a family? Wouldn't you have to check with your mum?'

'I'm not a kid,' retorted Maritsa. 'I'm nearly thirteen. And I've got no mama... Got a papa, but he's a professor, so he's much too busy.'

The woman said, 'What about your grannie? You'd have to ask her.'

Maritsa shrugged. '*Grand-mère* wouldn't mind. She could help, too. With the sewing and things.' Oh, why did they have to talk to her as if she was a kid? 'My gran's good at sewing and she knows all about puppets,' she lied pointlessly, knowing that her case was already lost.

'Then why not set up your own company, you and your grannie?' suggested the woman. 'You'd be competition for us. Bet you'd be good. Bet you'd be terrific!'

'Thanks,' said Maritsa. 'Thanks.' She walked rapidly away. A tear rolled down her cheek and she scrubbed at it furiously. Even though she'd given them all that money, she thought, they'd still treated her like a kid. And they hadn't even noticed her bare feet. They hadn't taken her seriously, like Wilhelm and his wife had. Wilhelm had *chosen* her: he'd said so. And he might be old and fat but he cared about her, cared about her sore feet. Wilhelm could *see* she had talent, that she could make it to the top...

At the foot of the escalators, a woman grabbed her roughly. 'Where's my daughter, gypsy filth?' Her fingernails hurt.

Maritsa looked and saw it was Sylvie's mama, no longer passive but weeping and angry.

'Where's my daughter?' she kept shouting. 'Where's my little girl?' The HOMELESS placard hung skewed across her chest.

'I told you,' yelled Maritsa. 'She went to see a friend.'

The woman wrenched at a fistful of Maritsa's hair. 'Tell me who!' she screamed.

Maritsa suddenly spotted Marcel. 'You tell her!' she screamed. 'Tell your mama the truth!'

But Marcel was too frightened to utter a word.

CHAPTER ELEVEN

People paused. People stared.

'Go on! Hit her, *madame!*' someone joked. 'Give us a good fight!'

A busker with a guitar case slung over his back pushed his way in, shepherding the three of them to one side. 'You're in everyone's way,' he said. 'Someone's going to get hurt.'

It was Paul.

The woman became suddenly docile, defeated. She looked at Maritsa and her eyes swam with tears.

'Tell me,' she pleaded. 'Please. You've *got* to know something.'

But Maritsa was trembling too much to speak.

'What's it all about?' asked Paul. The woman told him. 'I see,' he said thoughtfully. 'And you think Maritsa knows something?'

Maritsa was amazed. He didn't call me gypsy, she thought, he remembered my name.

The woman looked desperate. 'The gypsy was out there with Sylvie. I saw them go.'

Paul frowned. 'Maybe she's gone window-shopping,' he suggested. 'Enough trendy places up there. Kids do wander,' he added comfortingly.

'Not my Sylvie. My Sylvie's a good girl.'

Marcel began snuffling. The woman seemed to notice him for the first time. She picked him up. 'He's worn out,' she said. 'We should have gone to his gran's place hours ago, but we can't leave without his sister.'

Paul spoke to Marcel. 'What happened? Can you tell us?'

Marcel pointed. 'That gypsy called Sylvie a gagdet.'

'That's awful!' Paul looked suitably shocked. Then he turned to Maritsa. 'Did Sylvie tell you where she was going?'

'To see a friend,' wailed Maritsa (it was only half the secret). 'I *told* you!'

The woman eyed her balefully. 'What friend? She hasn't got any friends around here.'

'I don't know,' wept Maritsa.

'Tell you what,' said Paul. 'We ought to talk to those people upstairs. They could keep an eye out for her.'

The woman looked suspicious. 'What people upstairs?'

'In the ticket office,' explained Paul. 'Up there, they've got cameras and screens – I've seen them. And don't you think the station staff might want to know about a missing girl?'

'The station staff?' The woman laughed harshly. 'They'd cheer! One less of us makes them very happy.' Even so, she allowed Paul to escort them upstairs.

Still trembling, Maritsa fled back to Rose.

She found her rummaging through one of her bulging bags, pulling out boxes, fussing over a tangle of silky stuff, a glittery brooch, a miscellaneous collection of pens and pencils, a grubby exercise book and big, old-fashioned alarm clock.

Maritsa hung about.

'I've come back,' she said at last.

'So I see,' Rose grunted. Then she peered at Maritsa over the top of her spectacles. 'You're a bad girl,' she said.

It was too much. Maritsa began to cry again. 'It wasn't my fault that kid ran away.'

'Kid? What kid?'

When Maritsa told her, she sniffed. 'Should have been at school,' she muttered, 'or with her *maman*, not hanging round parks, getting herself into trouble.'

But Sylvie'd talked about a boyfriend, Maritsa remembered. He'd take care of her, wouldn't he? Maybe she'd got fed up, always having to look after her little brother, maybe she'd gone after something more exciting...

Like a screen test, she thought and a little curl of excitement made her shiver.

'I met a man in the park,' she confided. 'He makes films. He thinks I could be a star.'

Rose glanced at her sharply. 'Men are only after one thing, my girl,' she warned. 'Even that nice young man who brought me a sandwich.'

'Paul?' Maritsa blushed. 'He's not after anything.' Paul might be dishy, she thought, but he was too old. And a *gadjo*...

Anyway, the mama had started hinting at a marriage deal. Some time in the future... If things didn't work out, she might even go back. Might it have been that dishy boy she'd fancied in the country, she wondered? Or someone boring? Real love was like a fire, the songs said, burning, burning, eating you up.

And she wanted to live, be a star, choose her own men...

'You should go back to your mama,' said Rose unexpectedly.

'Haven't got...'

'I know, I know.' Rose looked troubled. 'I'm a silly old woman, I forget things...' She pulled out a threadbare silk scarf with a big, splashy print. 'Mop yourself up, *mademoiselle*.' Then awkwardly, as if she'd never done such a thing before, she put an arm around Maritsa's shoulders.

Maritsa blinked. 'I'm not bad.'

'Of course you're not.' Rose was rummaging again. 'Look, I've got something for you.' She brought out a couple of books and dumped them in Maritsa's lap. 'These belonged to your papa,' she said.

Maritsa cradled them, running her fingers over the gold letters. Then she shook herself. She was believing it too.

'You're fibbing,' she said. 'You're not really my gran, so your son couldn't have been my papa.'

Rose sighed. 'He wasn't anyone's papa,' she said sadly. 'He was only a baby...'

A train came in. People got out, stepping warily round Rose's spread-out possessions.

'Look at all that mess,' complained a girl.

The old woman stood up shakily, leaning hard on Maritsa'a shoulder. 'I beg your pardon, *mademoiselle*?'

The girl looked taken aback. 'Oh, pardon me, I'm sure.'

'I should think so too,' thundered Rose.

Maritsa giggled behind her hand. '*Grand-mère*, you're great!'

'I'm not your *grand-mère*,' said Rose. 'You just said so.'

Then Maritsa threw her arms around her. 'Oh yes you are,' she said. She sat down beside her. 'Where is he now?'

Rose looked puzzled. 'Where's who?'

'Your baby,' said Maritsa. 'Your son. My papa.'

'He died,' said Rose vaguely. She was silent for a moment. 'He'd have been a clever one if he'd grown up, just like his grandfather...' Then she drew close. 'I make him up,' she confided, 'the way he might have been been. A professor, a doctor...' She picked up one of the books. 'If the world treats you badly, you can always make up another one.'

Maritsa grinned. 'That's what the fairy godmother said!'

Rose shook her head. 'Fairy godmothers, at your age!' She

opened one of the books. 'Time you made a start on a new story, young lady.' She put her finger on the first line. *'Once there was a woman who longed for a child...'* but soon she grew drowsy and began stumbling over the words.

Maritsa looked at the pages. She wanted more story.

She prodded the old woman. *'Grand-mère!* Wake up!'

Rose mumbled something, then slumped.

Maritsa caught the book as it slithered down and pushed it, along with the others, into one of the bags. As she moved away, the old woman stretched herself out across the seats, taking up all the space. Maritsa carefully removed her funny, lopsided spectacles and tucked those away too.

Then she sat on the ground and opened her own book, but the other one seemed much more exciting now. She reached over, pulled it out again and tried to read it, but it was much too difficult.

At last, bored, she went off to see if Paul was still around, to see if there was any news.

She heard him before she found him, playing his guitar and singing some American song. When he spotted her in the crowd, he shook his head slightly.

No.

That meant Sylvie hadn't come back.

Maritsa didn't care. That girl was a pain, so good riddance.

She was sorry for little Marcel, though, who'd been badly scared. She was even sorry for Sylvie's mama, but Sylvie? No. She'd turn up. She was having fun...

She squatted against the wall until Paul had finished his act, enjoying the music and the sound of the strange, foreign words. She might go to America one day, she thought. Hollywood. That man Wilhelm might send her.

She remembered the puppets, how much she'd longed to join that company and how they'd treated her like a kid. She pushed the memory away. No money in it, the woman had said, so who wanted that? With Wilhelm, there'd be pots of money. Hadn't he told her so?

But he might have been lying. Lying seemed to go with a man with no eyes.

She could talk to Paul about it, she thought suddenly. Talking to Rose was a waste of time, but Paul was streetwise and sensible. A busker. He'd know.

She waited.

The guitar was finally unplugged and stowed away. 'She hasn't turned up,' said Paul. 'Are you sure you don't know anything more?'

Maritsa felt irritated. Sylvie again. Always Sylvie, with her pretty fair hair and her neat pink hairslide. 'I could tell you about me,' she said, 'but you wouldn't listen, would you?'

Paul took two apples out of his pocket. 'Try me.' He gave one to Maritsa. 'It's not much,' he said. 'And the snack bar's closed. Want to eat outside?'

She was tempted. 'But it's late,' she said. 'And they mightn't let me back in. And there's my gran down there.'

'Then eat your apple here.'

Maritsa bit into it, juice running down her chin. 'I met a man,' she boasted. 'He wants to put me in a film.'

Paul looked interested. 'Sounds great,' he said slowly. 'So what's the problem?'

'I don't like him,' said Maritsa.

'You can't like everyone you work for,' said Paul. 'What's wrong with him?'

'He's got no eyes.'

Paul looked amazed. 'You mean he's blind?'

'He wears mirrors where his eyes ought to be. And mirrors steal people's souls; they stole pictures of me...' She paused. He was only a *gadjo*, after all; what would he understand about things like that? 'And he took some,' she added awkwardly.

Paul frowned, working it out. 'You mean with a camera too?'

Maritsa nodded.

'Then you've been to his studio, so you know he's all right.'

'He took them in the park,' said Maritsa. 'And he never asked.'

'In the park? Which park?'

'The Luxembourg Gardens.' She told him the rest of the story, about Wilhelm's wife, about the Café Laure.

'So. Tell me what he looks like, this Mr Wilhelm.'

Maritsa did.

'And Mrs Wilhelm?'

That made her giggle but she told him: the glossy peach-blonde hair, the plum-varnished nails, the crystal drop earrings and those wonderful black-buttoned silver leather boots that Maritsa would have liked for herself.

Paul went very quiet.

Then he nodded slowly, as if he'd just made up his mind about something important. 'It's a fantastic piece of luck, isn't it,' he said, 'for a gypsy kid like you...'

Maritsa felt angry – she was no kid. And he should have said no. He should have reminded her of his stories about girls disappearing. After all, Sylvie had disappeared.

'You think I should turn up, then?' Perhaps he didn't really care. She was only a gypsy. Perhaps he was only concerned about pretty little blonde girls who brushed their hair.

'To the Café Laure? Whyever not?' He shrugged. 'I know that place – it's OK. And a chance like that – I mean, it's too good to miss out on.'

'Then you think I should do it?' Maritsa repeated.

Paul slung his guitar over his shoulders and struggled to his feet. 'Yes, I do.' He looked down at her gravely. 'Why not go tomorrow,' he said, 'while you're still feeling brave?'

'I was going to anyway,' retorted Maritsa. 'I don't need you to tell me – I just thought you'd like to know. And I *always* feel brave,' she added.

'Well, I don't,' said Paul. He rested his hands on her shoulders for a moment. 'Good luck,' he said. 'And when you're a star, I'll be your number-one fan!' he promised as he walked away.

Maritsa shrugged and went back to Rose. The last train had just left, leaving behind its smell of smouldering ash.

The old woman was quite still for once, breathing almost imperceptibly. Maritsa lay down alongside the three seats, tucking her bag behind her head. Not for much longer, she told herself. Soon there might be a soft bed, even a little room...

A mouse scuttled up the side of the platform. It sat up, studying her, sniffing at the air. She threw it her apple core. So much for good blokes, she thought. Paul didn't care. His sexy green eyes and his friendliness didn't mean much more than the good-looking face and trendy jacket of the yob who'd tormented her. They were all *gadjé*, even the buskers *and* not to be trusted. So what if Wilhelm was old and ugly? He couldn't help that. And at least he was offering something. And that pretty lady must have found something good about him or she wouldn't have married him.

There was only one way to find out about Wilhelm and she would have to take it. If it was a big mistake, she was tough, wasn't she? She could bite, she could kick. And she could run a lot faster than any fat middle-aged bloke.

But if Paul's hunch was right, she might end up a star after all and the mama and the *kumpania*'d be so proud of her.

A star...

She grinned. Those boys would make a meal of it. No more taunts about her shameful mum. '*Maritsa? Oh, she's our blood sister*', they'd boast.

A star...

Maritsa's eyes closed and she drifted through dreams of a fairy-tale ball with a rock band playing and a ragged godmother with wings and a squashy velvet hat. Then the prince in purple velvet asked her to dance and she spun round and round and round while his mirrored glasses glittered darkly and his fat pink lips came close, the dark O between them smelling of chocolate caramel.

And she woke up screaming.

Chapter Twelve

And even when she opened her eyes he was still there. Staring down at her. Stout. Chewing. Dressed in purple.

No, blue. Cornflower blue. Workman's overalls. And the crown had turned into a uniform cap. 'What's all the noise about?' grumbled Bertrand.

Maritsa felt silly. 'Nothing,' she said.

He began marching about officiously, checking on things. 'Old lady all right?' he called out.

'How would I know?' yawned Maritsa. 'I was asleep.'

'You were yelling. I heard you.'

Maritsa felt her cheeks glowing pink. 'I must have been dreaming,' she mumbled.

Bertrand humphed and went back to Rose. 'Looks a bit flushed,' he said expertly. 'But then wrapped up in all that rubbish... It's stuffy down here. Air's bad.' He came over and frowned. 'Bad for you too. Why don't you go home?'

'I'll go when I'm ready.'

'Don't give me any of your tongue!' Bertrand sighed heavily. 'You make life difficult for everyone, hanging round here. Now that girl's gone missing...'

Maritsa jerked upright. 'That was nothing to do with me!'

Bertrand lifted his cap and scratched his head. 'People talk,' he said. 'And gypsies bring bad luck.' He took out a packet of chewing gum. 'Want a piece?' He stood, considering her. 'No, you had nothing to do with it,' he decided. 'You're not much more than a kid yourself, same as her.' He chewed thoughtfully. 'So why don't you scoot off home? Got no business hanging around down here.'

'Well, neither has she, then!' Maritsa pointed.

'You mean *Mademoiselle* Rose?' Bertrand looked uncomfortable. 'Ah, you got me there... Used to be a teacher, *mademoiselle* Rose. Taught me, if you can believe it. Got herself in the family way.' He rounded his hands over his already plump stomach. 'They threw her out. People did then.' He shook his head. 'We kids didn't care. We liked her. We gave her flowers, I remember... Someone told us she lost the baby. Then I met up with her down here. Must be twenty, thirty years.'

'She must have changed a lot!'

'A beggar... *Mademoiselle* Rose! A bag lady, down on her luck. I wouldn't have known her. But she knew me. She knew all her kids.' He suddenly became fierce. 'All this nonsense about her being your grannie...' and he picked up his broom and walked off. 'Tomorrow night, gypsy,' he yelled back, 'out you go!'

Maritsa rearranged herself but she couldn't get back to

sleep. She walked around, then sat, staring into the cavernous smile of the poster lady until the first train thundered in at half-past five.

She waited until the platform clock showed a seven and a three and a zero. Then she went in search of coffee and something to eat.

But when she saw Sylvie's mama sitting motionless at the foot of the escalators, she turned and fled. There were other stations. There were other snack bars.

She got on the next train that came in and sat for a long time, letting station after station pass. All night, she thought and Sylvie hadn't come back. Her mama must have left Marcel with his gran...

She got out at random, choosing badly – a station with no snack bar. She ran up the unfamiliar steps and found herself standing on a tree-lined island in the middle of a busy road. The gloom of the previous day had vanished and now the sunlight was creamy cold. It glittered on the black iron flowers that blossomed above the Métro sign and burnished the coat of the ginger dog sprawled over a crate beside the newspaper stand.

She crossed into a street full of cheap clothes shops. Cut-price garments spilled out into market displays. Billboards shrieked their wares in fluorescent orange, red and green. Maritsa looked up and down, but as far as she could see there were nothing but clothes shops.

She turned into a side street; a baker's would do, she thought. It was a steep, narrow street, lined on both sides with small fabric shops opening on to the pavement. Bales of corduroy and wool stood stacked outside and sample lengths and neatly folded remnants were swinging from awnings. Trestle tables vanished under a profusion of lace, broderie anglaise, silk jerseys, taffetas, rich satins and sugar-candy nets, and behind them, the interior of each little shop seemed to glow like an Aladdin's cave.

Maritsa forgot about Sylvie. She even forgot about breakfast. Never had she been in such a marvellous place. She lingered over each counter, running her fingers pleasurably over the fabrics. The ones she liked best were the ones with gold and silver threads for she loved things that twinkled and shone. She draped a piece of mauve and turquoise lurex against her chest, straining to see her reflection in a shop window. And she imagined herself in a slinky dress, in a jacket made of this wondrous stuff, and she sighed.

One day...

Maybe tomorrow, she thought, if her meeting with Wilhelm went well.

Nightmares were just bad dreams. They didn't really *mean* anything — that was just old women's talk. And Paul seemed to think she'd be all right...

She came across a stall stacked with nothing but cardboard boxes. Unable to read the labels, she opened each box and peeped inside. There were tiny twists of baby elastic in pale pink and blue. There were skeins of silk cords knotted together and bunched posies of silken tassels. There were embroidered flowers and sequined hearts and leftover scraps of coloured lace.

Then she spotted a boxful of assorted buttons. With a little 'oooh!' of delight, she began sifting through them and each time she let a handful slide through her fingers, new treasures appeared. Dreamily, she began picking out the ones she liked best, lining them up in order of merit.

An irritable woman looked up from her knitting. 'If you're not buying them, leave them alone.' She gave Maritsa a hard look. 'How many have you pinched? How many have you got in your pockets, gypsy?'

Maritsa made a rude gesture and moved away, but when she was safely out of sight, she stopped to gloat over the silver daisy button that lay in the palm of her hand. The woman had labelled her 'thief', she reckoned, so she might as well be one.

But the magic had gone and she still hadn't found a snack bar.

The street curved round steeply and joined a big road with

a park on one side. The park was really a high, grassy hill and on the very top stood an ivory palace, glittering against the cold blue winter sky. It was really a church, Maritsa knew that. She'd seen it before, on postcards and pictures and sometimes from a distance, floating on the skyline.

And at the place where the park joined the road, there was a pancake stall: Maritsa could smell it from where she stood. She dropped the daisy button into her bag and brought out a fistful of coins.

Enough. Plenty.

She crossed over and, blowing on her fingers, she ordered three pancakes, hopping from foot to foot to keep warm, while the man slowly ladled out the batter then wrapped each pancake in its twist of paper.

'Going to eat that lot yourself?' he asked, wiping his fingers on the apron knotted round his ample waist.

And when Maritsa nodded, he smiled admiringly. '*Bon appetit!* Enjoy them!'

'Thank you,' said Maritsa. 'I will.'

She bit into the first one as she pushed open the little swing gate that led on to the hill. On her right there was a path that zigzagged lazily up the slope; on her left, broad steps and little terraces.

She chose the steps and began to climb. It was a long way

and her shoes were pinching. She longed to kick them off and climb barefoot but it was really too cold.

When she reached the second terrace she squatted against the rise of the step and finished the last pancake. She was almost on a level with the nearest rooftops and she could spy on the pancake seller, far below.

On the next terrace there was a small brown-skinned man twisting pieces of silver into decorative letters. Maritsa hung about, fascinated, watching him work.

'What's your name?' he asked without looking up.

'Maritsa.'

He twisted a piece of metal and flicked it with the pliers. Then he showed her a silver 'M'.

'That's for you.' He held out his hand. 'A hundred francs and a bit extra for the chain...'

It was beautiful and Maritsa wanted it.

'Can't afford it just now,' she said regretfully. 'But will you keep it for me? Can I buy it on my way back?'

'I'll make it eighty, then,' he bargained. 'Fifty, then. A special price, because I like you.'

Maritsa was tempted. Fifty francs was not much to give for something so pretty...

The man suddenly dropped the silver 'M' into her hand. 'A Christmas present, gypsy,' he said. 'Now I've crossed your palm with silver, will you bring me luck?'

'Oh yes,' breathed Maritsa. 'And thank you!' Luck was with her today, she thought, so she had plenty to spare.

She reached the top of the hill. Before her stood the church with its high domes dazzling in the sunlight and below lay the jumbled rooftops and twisty chimneypots of the old city. She walked over to the balustrade where a sprinkling of tourists were clustered round a telescope on a stand and a balloon seller stood, small and frail, under his big, bobbing parachute of silver.

She tried asking for money but nobody cared, so she found herself a bench under a canopy of frozen vines. Opening her hand, she gloated over the necklace, holding it so that the light made it sparkle, reluctant to fasten it around her neck where she could no longer admire it.

A stray cat stepped delicately along the rail, lifting its paws like a dancer. Why didn't it fall? Why didn't it get scared? She imagined herself on the same tightrope, her arms outstretched for balance, her feet leaving the ground, flying.

Flying...

She was flying on the end of a big silver balloon and the largest dome on the church was a scoop of ice cream. She put out her tongue and licked it and it tasted of vanilla.

From His shrine on the rooftop, Jesus gazed down at her in

gentle rebuke. 'This dome belongs to me, my child.'

Maritsa shrugged. 'A few small licks won't do it any harm.'

The next dome tasted of strawberries and cream.

Maritsa scooped it up with her finger. 'Yummy!' she cried.

The Madonna on the rooftop shifted her baby.

'That is *my* dome, gypsy. Strawberries and cream for my baby.'

'There's heaps left for your baby,' retorted Maritsa. 'There's plenty for everyone!'

Then the face of the Madonna flushed pinker than the dome. 'But I am the Queen of Heaven!' she declared and she pricked the balloon with her fingernail. 'Get down at once, you insolent beggar!'

And Maritsa went floating down, down, down and landed with a bump on the park bench. She opened her eyes, wondering where she could be.

A party of tourists came out of the church. Then Maritsa remembered. She slipped off her shoes and, tucking them into her bag, placed herself pathetically in their path.

'Oh you poor kid,' said a woman. 'And it's Christmas too,' and she pressed a couple of notes into Maritsa's hand.

A watchful priest hurried over, his black robe trailing. 'I cannot allow you to make use of the church steps for begging, my child,' he said. 'If you're hungry, go to the presbytery round the corner.'

Maritsa dropped the notes into her bag and left. She'd done quite well; there was no point in arguing. Down on the terrace, the jewellery maker looked up as she ran past. 'Don't forget that good luck, gypsy!'

She hung around the streets until mid-afternoon, until the church above her, on its hill, blushed pink as a wild rose. Then, at last, she found a baker's and picked up some chocolate *croissants* and buns to share with Rose.

As she crossed back to the island, the signs were beginning to be switched on above basement clubs: GIRLS GIRLS. GIRLS. Why not BOYS? wondered Maritsa. The woman at the newsstand poured some milky coffee from a Thermos, her slippered feet warmed by the sleeping dog. Maritsa glanced at her enviously; she would have liked a warm drink too.

But she could have one later, she thought.

Wilhelm could buy her one at the Café Laure...

Along the passageway she found Rose, huddled on a blanket, snoring. Maritsa crouched beside her and pounded gently on the soft mound of her back.

'I've got you some croissants.'

The old woman stirred and shook her head. 'Baker's closed,' she muttered. 'They always close at lunchtime. You know that.'

Maritsa laughed. 'It's ages past lunchtime, *Grand-mère.*'

'I'm not your grannie...' Rose eyed her fiercely. *'Grand-mère, Grand-mère*...have you fed the goat?'

Maritsa looked blank.

'It's your turn today, Suzanne. You promised.'

Maritsa giggled. 'I'm not Suzanne. You're dreaming.'

'Nonsense.'

'Who am I, then?'

Rose frowned, concentrated. 'You're that gypsy kid,' she said at last. 'The one who thinks I'm her gran.'

Maritsa gave up. 'Have a croissant.'

'Don't want a croissant.'

'They're chocolate ones. I bought them specially for you...'

'Not hungry.'

'Have you eaten anything at all?' asked Maritsa.

Rose looked at her disdainfully. 'Lunch,' she said. 'I had lunch.'

'What did you have?'

'I had lunch with Pierre,' said Rose dreamily. 'Shrimps with mayonnaise...'

Maritsa shuddered. 'Ugh, insects!'

'Almond trout,' Rose went on, ignoring her, 'a little green salad, lemon tart, iced champagne...'

'Oh, Rose! What did you really have?'

'I just told you.'

'The truth, Rose.'

Rose sniffed. '*I'm* not the one who tells the lies.'

Maritsa took one of the croissants out of its paper bag. She was very hungry. She ate a second one, watching Rose's face. Then she held out a third. 'This one's for you, *grand-mère.*'

But Rose wasn't interested. Perhaps she *had* eaten...

A group of people hesitated, threw coins, then went on walking. One of them looked a bit like Paul, but his clothes were all wrong and he wasn't carrying a guitar case. Maritsa sighed. It would have been nice to have spoken to Paul before she left, to have him wish her good luck.

She turned to Rose. 'I've got to go somewhere,' she said awkwardly. 'Wish me luck, *Grand-mère.*'

'You don't need luck,' said Rose primly. 'You need application.'

Maritsa walked down to the ladies' toilet, peeed, then studied her reflection in the mirror over the sink. She finger-combed her hair and tidied up her ribbons – those narrow gold bands looked so good with her earrings, she thought. She held up the necklace, admired the swinging silver M for the last time, then fastened it round her neck.

Finally, she scrubbed her face and hands with soap and water, drying them over the hot-air machine. She felt pleased with herself: she smelt good, she looked good and she carried her luck with her.

A star, she thought...

Then she left for the Café Laure.

CHAPTER THIRTEEN

There was no one begging at the foot of the escalators. And the homeless woman had vanished, along with the others.

Maritsa was relieved. Her luck was holding. It was a good omen. They must have found Sylvie. She must have turned up. She smiled secretly. Sylvie's mama would wallop her and didn't that girl deserve it!

Upstairs on the concourse, she found a fiddler playing tunes from home, tapping his foot so wildly he could have been dancing. Another good omen! She threw him a coin and he gave a wide, gap-toothed grin and said, in Rom, in the dialect her own people used, 'Good health, gypsy child and good fortune go with you.'

'Good health and good fortune,' she answered back.

So, cocooned in luck, Maritsa walked out into the jewelled night and found every car garnished with diamonds or rubies, Christmas fairy lights dancing in each black-veined tree-head and shop windows glowing like big golden icons.

But when she crossed the boulevard and began the long trek round the side of the park, the enchantment faded and something else took its place. It was nothing at first, just a feeling, just a prickling at the back of her neck. She turned round to prove that there was nobody there, that there was nobody following her, but the feeling persisted. Was someone blending too easily with the crowd? Turning a little too swiftly into a student or a tourist or one of those men out walking with his girlfriend?

Again she felt it and again she turned, but again the figure became indefinable. She stopped and checked a third time. Had she only imagined someone melting into the shadows?

She tried to concentrate. She needed to be cool. Wasn't she going for a screen test? Wasn't she going to be a star? The Café Laure, they'd said. On the other side of the park, but along which street? It had to be pretty obvious, or they'd have told her. It couldn't be too hard to find.

But after she'd passed the small car park, the dark tree clouds inside the Luxembourg Gardens seemed to be massing above her head, muttering and rustling and threatening vague evil. She remembered the heron and shivered. And again she sensed it. This time she ignored it. Of course there were people behind her, and why shouldn't there be? Weren't there always people in the streets of Paris?

Still, she was glad when she reached the main road on the other side of the park, with its bright lights and shops and cafés. She waited for a gap in the traffic, then darted across. At last she'd given that creep the slip, she thought (if he'd ever existed). Now she'd got rid of him...

And there on her right, the reassuring hulk of St Sulpice seemed to be telling her that everything was fine, that everything was OK, that she was going for a screen test, that she was just nervous, that she'd been imagining things.

Maritsa pulled her thoughts together. The Café Laure. *Where?*

She would have to ask.

In the small tobacco bar, a woman looked up from polishing glasses. 'No begging, if you please.'

'But I'm not begging,' said Maritsa, checking her reflection in the mirror with the clock. 'I'm looking for a place. I'm looking for the Café Laure.'

The woman shrugged. 'I can't help you there, *mademoiselle.*'

Maritsa ran into a clothes shop. The music was so loud that she had to shout.

'Café Laure?' yelled one of the women. 'Never heard of it.'

Outside she found a group of people huddled around maps and guide books.

'Café Laure?' she asked hopefully but they smiled and waved their arms about. '*Nein, nein...*'

She tried the chestnut man on the corner.

'Café Laure?' He pointed. 'Down there, *mademoiselle.* First right, then right again. Rue Platon.'

Maritsa thanked him and turned and suddenly felt her shadow turning too.

It had followed her across. It had been tracking her all the time.

She turned and ran at it, determined to confront it, prise whoever it was out of the crowd, give him a shape, a face, a name.

Someone slipped into a parked car, slammed the door, started the engine. Which car? Which car? She couldn't start banging on windscreens.

An anonymous vehicle moved into the stream of traffic. Maritsa stared, trying to pick it out. Now, headlights weren't diamonds any more, they were eyes, wide staring yellow eyes, hunters' eyes.

And she still had to find the Café Laure.

She ran round one corner, then another, trying to remember the chestnut man's instructions. She ran round the back of St Sulpice and out on to a strange boulevard. She was lost, she was angry and she was late for her rendezvous. That creep had spoilt everything and Maritsa cursed him.

He was probably nothing but a cheap *dragueur* – one of those blokes who pestered girls, hoping to find a cheap tart – but why pick on her?

Then miraculously, she caught sight of the silky beige coat and the black and silver boots.

'Hey!' she called. *'Madame Wilhelm!'*

The woman whipped round, recognized her, came back. 'Our little gypsy!' She parted her lips in a small coral smile. 'Coming to see us after all, dear? How nice. But why the gift-wrapped plaits?' She fingered the gold strands of the cake-box ribbons, flicked at a strand of the loose dark hair. 'I prefer it wild,' she murmured. 'Like this.' Then she pointed. 'There it is.'

The gold-scalloped awning that marked the empty terrace of the Café Laure was angled round the corner of the next street. 'So glad you found us,' the woman said, pushing open the coloured-glass door.

A breath of warm, tobacco-scented air enveloped them as they moved in out of the cold. Above the bar, a small television screen was running a noisy replay of a rugby match and between big arched mirrors, thickly varnished, yellowing posters of antique cars hung in glossy black frames.

With a small shiver of excitement, Maritsa followed her to a table by the window, where a teenage boy was flicking through the pages of a magazine.

'This is my nephew,' the woman said.

The boy ignored them.

The woman spoke to him sharply: 'Josef! Manners!' He

looked up languidly. 'Put that stuff away!' The facets of her ear-rings glittered under the orange light of the low-slung lamp. She smiled, became formal. 'Here's the gypsy kid I told you about. We met outside.' She turned to Maritsa. 'What did you say your name was, dear?'

'Maritsa. And I'm *not* a kid.'

'You speak very good French,' said the woman, 'consider-ing...'

Maritsa shrugged. Unlike the boys, she'd picked up French easily. One day, when she became a star, she'd pick up American too.

'What will you have, *Mademoiselle* Maritsa?'

Flattered, she asked for a coffee.

The boy ordered a cola.

Maritsa considered him. He was about fourteen, she guessed and almost good-looking, with deep-set grey eyes, pale skin and dark, slicked-back hair. But if only he didn't fidget so much; if only those long, slender fingers would stop fiddling with that small cold sore in the corner of his mouth, or pluck-ing at the scrolled pages of his magazine.

She unwrapped her sugar lump and dunked it in her coffee. She was about to pop it into her mouth when the woman said, 'Don't.'

Maritsa was surprised. 'Why not?'

'Bad for your figure. Don't want to put on fat...' The woman took a small folded packet out of her bag. 'Try some of this,' she said, shaking a white, sugary substance into Maritsa's coffee cup. 'Synthetic sweetener. Better for you than that stuff,' and she took the sugar lumps away. 'If you're going to be a star, dear, you need to start thinking about your shape.'

Maritsa stirred her coffee, then tasted it.

'It tastes funny,' she complained.

The woman nodded. 'But you'll soon get used to it.'

It's not bad, Maritsa decided and she drank thirstily, wiping the coffee moustache with the back of her hand. She would have to learn about things like that, she thought – being on a special diet, taking care of her body...

She began wondering when Wilhelm would turn up and if she would still find him evil.

'Where's your husband?' she asked.

The boy snorted.

The woman frowned at him. 'You mean Wilhelm? Oh, he's back at the studio.'

The boy took out small packet of cigarette papers and rolled himself a joint, stooping over the lighter flame so that, for an instant, his pallid face glowed. He held it out to Maritsa, but she shook her head. Then he turned to the woman. 'Same routine as the little blonde?'

The woman looked annoyed. 'How would I know?

Depends how much' — she suddenly glittered at Maritsa — '*talent* she's got.' She counted out a small stack of coins and placed
it over the bill, printed a neat coral O on the paper napkin and
stood up. 'Shall we be off, then?'

Maritsa felt suddenly confused. 'I thought the screen test
would be happening here.'

'Oh no, dear.' The woman held open the door. 'You need a
proper studio for that sort of thing.'

She led the way to a small blue Citröen parked in a side street.
When she pressed a control, the doors clicked and unlocked.

Maritsa was impressed. If ever she had a car, she thought,
she'd choose one that did that. She slid into the back, savouring
the smells and textures of someone else's world — the woman's
rich, heavy perfume and the powdery scent of the car freshener
that didn't quite disguise the odour of stale tobacco and other,
indefinable things. She ran her fingers over the smooth, blue-
grey moquette and the frilled satin cushions in the back. She
pressed a button by accident and discovered an ashtray and for
a while played at popping it in and out. Then she found the
toys — a couple of dolls, a woolly rabbit with a bow tie and a
nylon fur poodle with a red-felt tongue.

Maritsa picked up the poodle and cuddled it on her lap.
She'd never had any toys, even when she was a kid and the soft
fur was nice. A real puppy would be nicer, though, she thought.

Maybe, one day, she'd get one, share it with Rose. Begging with a dog would be great.

Rose...

'I'll have to get back to my gran,' she said sleepily. 'Afterwards...'

The woman started the car, switching on the radio at the same time. 'Don't you worry, dear,' she said, pouting into an illuminated vanity mirror. 'We'll run you back. The streets of Paris aren't safe for young girls at night.'

The boy made a strange choking sound and passed her the joint. This time Maritsa tried it, but it made her splutter and cough, so she handed it back.

He was odd, she thought, but she didn't care. She snuggled back, hugging the poodle, enjoying the music, already feeling like a star, watching the streets moving past, bright lamps blossoming like tall-stemmed flowers along the curve of the bridge, the cold glimmer of the glass pyramid outside the Louvre and the big gold-winged angels flying above the Opéra house. She gawped at the Christmas windows along the Boulevard Haussmann, under which (she knew) women from her *kumpania* would be sitting, begging with their collection of babies and all the time kept catching glimpses of the Eiffel Tower with its Christmas-tree glitter and the high, ice-cream domes of the Sacré Coeur.

Then they entered the ring road that curved round the edges of Paris and the familiar landmarks dissolved into a maze of lights. After a while, they left by one of the exits, drove alongside railway tracks, crossed over a canal, moved past the blinding dazzle of a football stadium and the sinister black void of a locked-up cemetery.

Maritsa yawned. 'Where are we?'

'Don't worry, dear,' said the woman. 'Not far now.' Beside her, the boy had begun twitching his thin shoulders in response to the radio. They drove through a place with locked-up factories and empty warehouses, past a small shopping arcade with escalators and into a housing estate built like a ship, with round side windows, like portholes and high walls painted in seasick swirls of colour.

The underground parking had portholes in its ceiling.

Maritsa blinked. 'Where?'

The woman turned round and smiled. 'The studio, dear. Up there. You'll see.' She walked round and opened the car door.

Maritsa stumbled out.

'I feel funny,' she said.

'Give her a hand, Josef,' ordered the woman. She patted Maritsa on the head. 'You're a bit carsick, dear,' she said, 'that's all.'

Maritsa staggered in her high, broken heels. She clutched uselessly at the boy, as disconcerted by his fragility as she was by her own light-headedness. They walked up the steps. After the stuffiness of the car, the outside cold was shocking.

And her head seemed crammed with tangled thoughts, unfinished sentences. *Grand-mère*, she thought. Got to get back to the Métro, to Luxembourg... But the lights above the main entrance started dancing in her eyes, round and round and round, reminding her that she was going to be a star, a star...

...if only that stupid *dragueur* would stop following her, pestering her...

Even now she could see the headlights of a car, his car, moving in to spoil things, slowing, turning, parking in the shadows under the trees, then closing its yellow hunter's eyes and waiting for its prey. She cuddled closer to the boy, yet his iron embrace, the skinny, leather-clad arm pressed round her shoulders, suddenly felt as menacing as the shadow.

The woman pressed a button and spoke into a grille. A lock was released with a buzz.

She pushed open the main doors.

'Here we are, dear, safe and sound.'

And as they moved inside, the doors swung heavily back, then closed behind them with a final click.

CHAPTER FOURTEEN

Wilhelm came out of a ground-floor flat.

'Ah, so,' he said and his fat lips curled into a teasing smile. 'The gypsy princess. The girl who pinches shoes.'

'That's not true,' said Maritsa, suddenly hating him. Him. Wilhelm. The shadow. The evil. It had been Wilhelm who'd been stalking her, scaring her, trapping her. And there wasn't any screen test. Now she knew, she understood.

But she was streetwise, wasn't she? Young, healthy and wicked, she could take care of herself, still get away, move a lot faster than this ancient pair. 'Got to go to my gran now,' she said thickly, trying to run, but the blue and grey floor swirls suddenly rose over her head and her cheek went crashing against the chilly mosaic.

Drowning, she was drowning...

The woman hauled her out of the waves. 'Oh, you bad girl,' she scolded. 'I think you must be drunk, Maria, Marita, whatever your name is. You'd better come in and sleep it off.'

'No,' protested Maritsa, but a firm arm was guiding her towards the door and her own legs went stumbling into a blaze of lights, even though she tried to stop them.

Lights, shuttered lights and a camera on a tripod.

But she no longer cared about being a star, she was tired, she just wanted to sleep, sleep...

And against the end wall, in a pool of light, she saw a mattress, with sheets that were rumpled, as if someone had just rolled out of them. She saw cream satin pillows and padded lace hearts threaded with sugar-pink ribbons.

A bed.

At last.

She stumbled over to it. The sheets were silky, the mattress soft and sagging.

Wilhelm snapped open a beer can, cracking something inside her skull.

'Look at that.' His voice seemed to boom from somewhere on the ceiling. 'She's a natural. I told you.' He laughed. 'These gypsy kids are anybody's.'

Maritsa was puzzled. *I'm not anybody's,* she thought. *I'm mine.*

The room receded, then came back at her in jagged sections – the rocking horse, the silver spotlights, the pink-shaded table-lamp, the bowls of sugared almonds, the fluffy toys. She remembered the poodle with the red-felt tongue.

'Where's my toy puppy?' she heard herself asking childishly.

The woman tossed her a fleecy rabbit. 'Try this one, dear. Just as good.'

The boy was acting strangely again, moving about above her, opening drawers and cupboards, tugging at the collar of the woman's silk shirt.

The woman's voice floated over Maritsa's head. 'No more fixes... ruins your performance...'

Performance. What performance? Who was going to perform?

And when were they going to do the screen test?

And what *was* a screen test? Maritsa didn't know.

Photographs – images stolen from strangers – began slowly rotating through the flowers on the wallpaper, shifting, displaying awful secrets: small children half-crushed by naked men, a blonde girl with blood running down her thighs, a girl on a carousel with skirts flying, a narrow slip of fabric half-concealing her sex...

A gypsy girl. *Herself.* Shameful, impure – what if the mama saw?

Maritsa pointed angrily. 'That's me.'

The woman shifted, clattered. 'That's right, dear. Sexy, isn't it?' Her shiny lips moved back over the edges of her teeth. 'But you'll have to show us a bit more than that if you're going to be a star.' Her earrings flashed lightning. 'Don't be shy. We're all friends here.'

Maritsa drew a breath and swallowed smoke, rich, sickly,

cutting her throat. Wilhelm loomed over her, the cigar a brown turd on his jutting lower lip. A petal of ash landed on her cheek and she scrubbed at it wildly – it was as if he'd already touched her. Helplessly, she pulled the sheet up over her head, hiding her face, locking herself away.

It was then that she saw it – the small, spreading bloodstain, the little scarlet flower on the crumpled silk.

Was that her own voice screaming? Or was it someone outside?

Screaming.

Shouting.

Yelling.

Banging at the door. Ringing the bell.

Too much noise, thought Maritsa and she turned her bruised cheek against the pillows and closed her eyes.

Too much noise.

Too much evil.

If you think the world is bad, the fairy had said, then make yourself a better one.

So Maritsa tried.

She began by looking for those theatre people, trying to pick out a pattern of red and blue stripes, a flash of sequins, a white woolly wig. Maybe they'd have changed their minds. It would be fun, she thought wistfully, painting the dolls, making the costumes, cutting out little pieces of glossy satin, ruffling net and sticking sparkly sequins on to gold-paper crowns. She could help them in other ways too: she knew such a lot about making money and carrying the takings in that box was just asking for trouble...

But what was Paul doing there, that nice busker Paul, bending over her, looking worried?

'I'm OK,' she said crossly. He was such a fusser, thought she was a kid, thought she couldn't take care of herself. It was Paul who couldn't take care of himself. There was far too much noise. He wouldn't make a centime tonight, better pack up, no one would ever hear his music with all that din.

The lousy police were already moving them on; the cops were always moving people on, never left them in peace. Her nose brushed against a fur coat hanging on the wall, its faintly animal smell laced with scent. She put her finger out and stroked it as she drifted past. Nice. Warm. Rose should have a fur coat, she thought, instead of those rotten old blankets... ·

Blankets. Rough. Scratching her chin.

'I'm not Rose,' protested Maritsa.

But the train was already moving off.

Work, she must work. She must make some money.

She got off at Opéra, a good place for a pitch. The platform was tiled in blue, rich as midnight, rich as the wallets of the theatre goers. She rode the escalators with the crowd, heard the ticket barrier click-clicking as they pushed through it.

Under the Christmas tree, the Arabs were playing some ancient carol. Maritsa wriggled to the front; she wanted to look at the drums again.

Someone hauled her back. 'You're anybody's,' he sneered, dropping cigar ash into her hair. Then his arm closed like a vice around her waist. 'You're mine.'

'No, I'm not!' She struggled free. Then she spat and stood, watching the frothy ball of spittle rolling slowly down the front of his padded green jacket.

'Police!' she heard him shout.

A police siren...

Police! Police!

Maritsa dived into the crowd. She could still hear him shouting: 'That gypsy! She's a thief! Stop her! She stole those shoes...'

Maritsa stepped out of the shoes and ran up the steps. Bare feet were better for begging, everyone knew that. The little snack bar at the top was sparkling with tinsel, but the shops on either side had their green shutters closed. Down below, the music had started again and she paused, looking back.

Then, out of the crowd, came a strange figure – a three-cornered hat, a patchwork of scarlet and gold, a kaleidoscope of coloured ribbons and a tinkling of bells. It skipped across the polished floor. It danced up the steps. It danced rings round Maritsa. Its eyes were little stars and its mouth was all laughter.

Maritsa started to giggle. 'Go away,' she cried and it vanished.

She ran after it, but outside there were so many other things to see.

For the bare trees along the Boulevard Haussmann were frosted now and starred with little lights and across the street the floodlit dome of the opera house glowed against an inky sky. And there, in the windows of the Galeries Lafayette, multi-coloured planets rotated among glittery glass stars and orange cellophane suns. And there were jewel-eyed birds with electronic crests and wings that really moved and golden-scaled monsters with sequined eyes and a spaceman offering gifts to a green-haired princess.

Then Maritsa saw the women sitting under the lamppost, flowered cotton skirts over sturdy gypsy legs, sleeping babies tucked snugly inside flowered shawls, the fabric turned back to show off their slumbering faces.

'Maritsa! Hey — Maritsa!'

She tried to ignore them.

'They're crazy with worry about you. The boys sulk all day — everyone's saying it's their fault.'

Maritsa stared at the pavement. She hadn't thought anyone would really *miss* her. She was just another mouth to feed, they kept telling her that.

'No, you're not,' said a voice from above her head and she saw a red and yellow shoe dangling from the lamppost.

'Come back for Christmas, at least.'

She was tempted. Yes. Christmas with the *kumpania...* outside, chickens roasting, spitting juice into the fire, the blokes drinking, singing, dancing, showing off, a pony whinnying and kids larking about. As usual, she'd be helping the women set the 'tables for God' under canvas lit with looped strings of naked bulbs, laying out rough, home-made bread, cans of beer and plates piled high with biscuits and cakes. She'd wait impatiently until the men had finished eating and then tuck in, the rich meat juices running down her chin, the little cakes crumbling deliciously inside her mouth.

And afterwards, inside the warm, steamed-up caravan, there'd be the TV chattering, the warm, soapy smell of drying clothes, new posies of plastic flowers under the picture of the Virgin, potted candles flickering ruby under St Sara-la-Kali and on the wall her stepdad's precious fiddle that had belonged to his grandad, just waiting to be played.

But the same old things? The same old life?

'It doesn't have to be, you know.' This time she saw the red and yellow legs twined round the stem of the lamppost. 'Depends on your point of view.'

Tendrils of curly white hair wreathed the three-cornered hat and the clown's smile was gummy.

But she had Rose, remembered Maritsa. *Grand-mère.* She couldn't go back. She had to look after Rose...

...and she floated past the windows of Monoprix, drifted past the lavender seller with his little brown donkey and his rough chunks of olive oil soaps...

...and she reached the main entrance of the second big store and there, on the other side of the glass, lay a cave with goblins and fairies, like one of the pictures in Rose's old books. And after that there was a forest with foxes and badgers and owls and mice and a hill with shepherds gazing at a flight of angels and a procession of people in old-fashioned clothes trudging through the snow, led by a white-haired clown in red and yellow who kept turning cartwheels.

...and she followed the three kings to the stable in the last window and there was the Madonna, her blue dress twinkling with gold threads, showing off her baby just like the women outside the Galeries Lafayette. Well, *she* didn't need any money, Maritsa thought, with all those angels playing trumpets and things and those rich kings with their presents and those ice-cream domes on the Sacré Coeur. Such a lot of fuss, she thought, over one small baby...

Someone was undressing her, taking her clothes off, even her knickers. She tried to fight them, biting, clawing.

'I'm *mine*,' she said fiercely. '*Mine*. You can't touch me.'

But angels in white hats moved calmly above her and hands that were gentle were stroking her head. 'It's all right, Maritsa. You're safe now.'

And there, on the ceiling, hovered the yellow and scarlet clown.

'You forgot your book,' he was saying.

She ignored him.

'Pity,' he sighed. 'You were almost able to read it.'

'I can read well enough.'

The clown flew down to the trolley the angels were pushing and stood on his head.

'You can't spell, though.'

'Can!'

'Can't.'

'*Can!*'

'Application!' He turned the right way up again. 'Big girl like you ought to be able to read and write.' He held out his hand. 'Coming?'

'Where?'

'You'll see...'

They flew through the big arched windows and out over the street. Down in République, the gaudy club signs were softened by falling snow and the glow from restaurants in the Place des Vosges scalloped the white arcades with orange half-moons. Outside the Centre Pompidou, a solitary fire-eater performed to a scant and frozen crowd, breathing a tongue of yellow flame into the frozen night. Maritsa clapped and he rotated wildly, looking up for his admirer through the curtains of snow.

Maritsa saw a snow crown growing on the golden head of Jeanne d'Arc and a little lace cap springing between the ears of her horse. She looked and saw snow whirling in rings round the lamps in the Tuileries Gardens. Then she rose dreamily through the falling snow, higher and higher, over the big jewelled sword that was the Champs-Elysées, over the loops of the diamond-black river, over the bobbing boats and bridges brilliantly graffiti'd with the lights of cars.

And inside the glass bauble, the great tower was a Christmas tree and Maritsa was the fairy standing at the top.

She spread out her flowered skirts.

'I'm a star,' she boasted.

'I know,' said the clown.

'And I don't need Wilhelm.'

'Who needs Wilhelm?' said the clown. 'Not even his mother.'

Then Maritsa looked at the city spread out below her, twinkling like a brooch and she picked it up and pinned it to her purple velvet blouse.

'All mine,' she sighed. 'All for me,' and the clown nodded approvingly.

'I'll get that little room with the bird in a cage...'

'But of course.'

'And a pair of American jeans and cowboy boots and a jacket with sequins...'

'Naturally.'

'And when I'm rich,' she said. 'I'll give a party for all the beggars and homeless people in Paris! And there'll be champagne and fireworks...'

'I'll be there,' said the clown.

'And I'll fly in an aeroplane,' said Maritsa. 'And take my gran along too.'

'If you want to fly in an aeroplane,' said the clown, 'do it.'

'And one day I'll read all of Rose's old books...'

'Application,' said the clown, suddenly prim.

'Oh, Rose,' giggled Maritsa.

'Don't be familiar,' grumbled the clown. '*It's mademoiselle* to you, young lady. *Mademoiselle, if* you please.'

CHAPTER FIFTEEN

Maritsa opened her eyes and saw Bertrand in a big navy-blue jacket and Rose tucked up in a wheelchair, cuddling her two precious bags.

She was still dreaming, she thought.

Then she pushed herself upright against the pillows and felt the laundered folds of a brushed-cotton nightie. 'Where?' she asked.

'Hospital for Sick Children,' said Bertrand. 'Rue de Sèvres.'

'But I'm not a child. And I'm not sick.' Maritsa turned to Rose. 'How did you get here, *Grand-mère*?'

The old woman looked pleased with herself. 'They had to bring me,' she boasted. 'We *drove*.' She began trying out the wheelchair, backing it against the screens.

A nurse stepped briskly through the gap. 'Careful, *madame*,' she scolded. 'We need that chair.' She rearranged the screens around the bed. Then she winked at Maritsa. 'We had to bring her up,' she explained. 'Police orders.'

Police? Maritsa was alarmed.

'Where did you put my clothes?' she demanded sharply.

'In the locker room downstairs,' said the nurse. She sighed.

'All those pretty petticoats...'

'And my shoes?'

'Those too.'

'Have the police looked in there?'

The nurse looked puzzled. 'Well, no. Why should they?'

'Someone called?' Paul pushed his head between two of the screens. Then all of him came in. 'She's awake, then?' He sat down on the edge of the bed. 'That was a long sleep,' he said.

Maritsa closed her eyes wearily. It was like the puppet show: who'd pop up next? Then she shivered. It might be them. That woman. That boy. And (oh, Madonna!) Wilhelm, leering at her, touching her...

She felt him already stroking her cheek and she slapped out. 'I'm *mine*,' she hissed. 'Don't touch me!'

'Easy, Maritsa... you're safe now.'

She opened her eyes and there was Paul.

'You're a wicked man,' Rose was saying. 'She's right to hit you. You've got her into enough trouble as it is.'

'Oh, Rose, that's not fair.'

The old woman glowered at Paul. '*Mademoiselle* to you, young man.'

'*Mademoiselle*, then. Look — we *had* to do it.'

'You used her. Why her?' Rose suddenly seemed larger than life. 'Why pick on her?'

Paul sighed. 'It was a risk we had to take.'

'You wouldn't with your own kind,' said Rose drily.

'We got Sylvie back.'

'Oh, I knew that,' Maritsa put in airily.

Paul seemed amazed. 'But how? We only found her after we'd picked you up.'

'Well, her mama wasn't there...' She changed the subject. 'Listen, Paul,' she whispered urgently. 'The cops are around and I did pinch those shoes.'

'What shoes?'

'Those fancy shoes. They're with my stuff in the locker room.'

Paul looked uncomfortable. 'Maritsa,' he said, 'I've got something to tell you. The cops – they're me. And some of my mates.'

Maritsa stared at him. Paul was a busker. A beggar, like herself. More lies, she thought. It was funny – once they got started, they never seemed to stop.

The nurse came in with cups of herb tea and a plate of little cakes. She gave a cup to Maritsa, helping her balance it between her hands. 'Drink it all up,' she said sternly, 'or there'll be trouble.' She looked across at Rose. 'What about the old lady? Does she take sugar?'

Rose glared at her, furious. 'The *old lady* could teach you some better manners, *mademoiselle.*'

Maritsa bit into a *petit four.* 'Stop fibbing, Paul,' she said. 'You can't be a cop. Cops don't play guitars. Cops don't busk.'

'Some of us do.'

Maritsa drew back. 'Well I think that's cheating.'

Bertrand had had enough. 'Listen, gypsy,' he said, pushing back his cap. 'Kids were disappearing. Kids like you – strays that no one gave a fig for. You ought to be grateful.'

Rose heaved herself upright. 'Leave the room, Bertrand Leblanc.' She pointed. 'At once.'

And Bertrand seemed to shrink inside his big woolly coat. *'Pardon, mademoiselle...'*

'At once, I said. Go!'

And Bertrand slunk away. 'The things I've done for her,' they heard him muttering. 'Finished. All finished. First thing in the morning, out she goes...'

'Oh, no!' cried Maritsa.

Paul grinned. 'I wouldn't worry. She's got Bertrand under her thumb. Haven't you, Rose?'

'Mademoiselle,' corrected Rose.

'It's true, though,' said Paul. Then he turned back to Maritsa. 'And I really am a cop. Do you mind?'

Maritsa shrugged. She felt confused. 'Dunno,' she muttered.

'Listen,' said Paul urgently. 'There's this group of people.

Making sex films with children. Nasty stuff, but lots of money in it.' He suddenly looked apologetic. 'Do you understand what I'm saying?'

Maritsa was offended. 'Of course I do. I'm not a kid.'

'They were using kids,' said Paul, 'then dumping them. Sometimes worse, much worse... We're only just beginning to find out. And they're tightly organized, like a bloody army – try breaking their security! They've got contacts, safe houses, code-words, websites. And they're all over the place – in big cities, where' – he glanced nervously at Rose – 'there are lots of girls like you. And they never use force. Children seek them out.' He paused. 'To people like you and Sylvie...'

'Sylvie?'

'...they told fairy tales about being a star.'

'Oh, I didn't *really* believe all that stuff.'

'Well, your friend Sylvie did... So, you see, we could never pin them down. Then you talked to me about this guy who'd offered you a screen test.'

'Why were you busking?' demanded Maritsa.

Paul looked embarrassed. 'To pick up information.'

'Well, that's not fair,' said Maritsa. 'That night – I thought we were friends.' She remembered something. 'Where are they now? Where's Wilhelm and Mrs Wilhelm?'

'Well, our friend Wilhelm's locked up in a rather special

hotel, while we try to find out more about him and his friends.'

'And his wife?'

'Oh, Chloe wasn't his wife.' Paul grinned. 'And there won't be any beauty treatments where that lady's going.'

'And Josef?'

Paul sighed. 'They did a real job on him. Been with them for ages. Got him hooked on hard drugs. He'll do anything for a fix and I mean *anything*. It'll take a long time...'

'Poor Josef,' said Maritsa. 'He won't like it in prison.'

'He's not going to prison,' said Paul. 'He needs treatment, not punishment. Maybe we can even track down his family.'

Maritsa was silent.

'I thought you beat people up,' she said at last. 'I thought you *liked* sending people to prison.'

'Some of us do.'

'But not you.'

'I do my best.'

Maritsa tested him. 'I really did pinch those shoes.'

Paul frowned. 'That was wrong.'

She waited. Was that all?

'No prison?'

He laughed. 'Don't be daft!' Then he suddenly thought of something. 'Is that what Wilhelm told you?'

Maritsa nodded. 'But he didn't fool me.'

'The rat!' muttered Paul. He put his cup back on the trolley, tiptoeing past Rose, who'd fallen asleep.

Maritsa was still working it out. 'Was that you, last night? Following me?'

Paul looked worried. 'I thought I was good.'

'Not good enough,' crowed Maritsa, 'to fool a gypsy.' She paused, thinking back. 'But Sylvie said she had a boyfriend.'

'She probably did.'

'You mean — Josef?'

'What do you think?'

She nodded slowly. 'He was cool,' she said, 'in an creepy sort of way. And he said this thing about a routine with a little blonde.'

Paul was looking at her with an odd expression.

'Where is Sylvie?' she asked him.

He was slow to answer.

'She's here,' he said at last.

'Can I go and visit her?'

'No.' Again the strange, frightening silence.

'Why not?' she asked, but she already knew.

'Sylvie was hurt. They — Wilhelm, the boy, or one of their customers — hurt her terribly. She's going to take a long time to get better.'

Maritsa remembered the brushed fair hair, the little pink

clips and the nice blue jumper. Sylvie was silly, she thought, but she didn't deserve that.

Whatever 'that' was. The terrible thing.

She had to know. She had to ask.

'They raped her?'

Paul's face set in grim anger. 'And they did it brutally.'

Maritsa was shocked. 'But she's only a kid!'

'So are you,' said Paul.

'No, I'm not!' protested Maritsa.

Paul looked solemn. 'Then you had Wilhelm well fooled...'

The nurse came back.

She looked at Maritsa's pale face. 'You're wearing her out,' she said. 'Time's up, police or no police.'

Paul got up. 'I'll be back in the morning to take you home,' he said. 'And I don't mean the Métro.'

'What about my gran?'

'She can come for the ride. She seems to enjoy being driven round in police cars.'

'You don't know where I live.'

'I will when you tell me.'

Rose woke with a start. 'Where am I?' she muttered.

Maritsa climbed out of bed and gave her a hug. 'At the hospital, *Grand-mère.*' She pointed at Paul. 'He'll tell you. He'll take you back.'

Rose fumbled about in her bags, then pulled out a picture book. *'Cinderella,'* she sniffed. 'Big girl like you...' She brought out a couple of other books and gave them to Maritsa.

'You'd better take care of these. Keep you out of mischief.'

'Oh, thank you, *grand-mère.'*

The lights came on as the nurse pushed away the screens and Maritsa found she was in a small ward, with paper streamers looped between beds and cots and a Christmas tree twinkling in one corner.

Paul and Rose joined the small exodus of afternoon visitors.

'Application!' she heard Rose saying as he pushed the wheelchair through the swing doors.

A woman with a little boy left the straggling procession and ran up to the nurse. 'She's over there, isn't she?' she said, pointing.

It was Sylvie's mama.

The nurse looked meaningfully down at her watch.

'Oh, let me thank her,' begged the woman. 'You don't understand...' and she darted across and gave Maritsa a hug. 'I was horrible and you were such a brave girl!'

Maritsa felt confused. She hadn't done anything.

Sylvie's mama scooped up a reluctant Marcel. 'Give the gypsy a kiss,' she said. 'She saved your sister's life.'

But Marcel hung back. 'Don't like gypsies.'

The woman smacked him on the bottom, then wiped his

nose. 'What do you know?' she said. 'You're just a baby. Gypsies are every bit as good as you and me.' Her eyes filled with tears as she turned back to Maritsa. 'I'd buy you something,' she said. 'Chocolates, anything, but I haven't got the cash.'

'How's Sylvie?' asked Maritsa awkwardly.

The woman looked bitter. 'She's alive.'

'I'll go and see her when she's feeling a bit better,' said Maritsa.

'Time's up,' the nurse insisted.

'Oh, would you?' said the woman. 'She'd like that. Oh, you're such a good girl.'

Maritsa picked up the books that Rose had left. They'd been too difficult before, but she'd learn. She traced the gold letters and looked at the pictures on the covers. Then she opened one and there, on a blank sheet, she saw the words.

And she could *read* them:

To Maritsa.
With love.
Grand-mère

She checked inside the second book and there it was again.

She turned to the girl in the next bed. 'Hey! Look what my gran gave me,' she said, holding up one of the books.

The girl smiled wanly, then closed her eyes.

She called the nurse: 'Come and see what I've got!'

'Sorry,' said the nurse. 'It'll have to wait for this good soup and cheese and vanilla ice cream...'

And Maritsa suddenly found she was hungry.

CHAPTER SIXTEEN

When Paul arrived the next day, Maritsa was already dressed, sitting in a spread of crumpled skirts, her bag, bulging with Rose's books, propped up beside her.

He looked down questioningly at the scuffed, grey and black trainers.

'Those other shoes got broken,' she explained. 'The heels came off, so we put them in the dressing-up box.' She started playing peek-a-boo with a toddler in bandages. Then she turned back to Paul.

'Can I see Sylvie?'

Paul shrugged. 'It isn't for me to say.' He went over to the desk and spoke to the nurses.

They whispered, then nodded. 'But not for long.'

One of them came back with him. 'She's still a very sick girl, remember,' she said to Maritsa. 'Still shocked. She may not want to see you.'

'That's OK.'

Maritsa followed her along the corridor to a single room. The nurse put her head round the door and called out softly: 'Sylvie?'

There was no reply.

The nurse tiptoed inside. 'Look,' she said. 'I've brought your gypsy friend.'

'Go away,' said Sylvie.

The nurse turned helplessly to Maritsa. 'It's early days,' she whispered. 'We can't push things...' But Maritsa had slipped past her into the room.

Sylvie buried her head in the pillows. 'Go away, gypsy.' Her voice sounded cracked and tearful. 'You bring bad luck.'

'They've got that man, Wilhelm,' said Maritsa. 'That woman too.'

'I don't care.'

'And there are more of them. Maybe they'll catch those as well.'

Sylvie turned round. Her eyes were pink from weeping. 'And you gave them the clue,' she taunted bitterly. 'Weren't you clever!'

'No, I wasn't,' said Maritsa. 'I thought I was going for a screen test, like you. That man Paul followed me.'

'He's a cop,' sniffled Sylvie. 'Cops are all the same.'

'No, they're not,' said Maritsa. 'They're all different. Like gypsies, like you lot. Some of them are nice and some of them are horrible.' She touched Sylvie's arm. 'Does it still hurt, what they did?'

'How would you know?'

'I saw those photos...' Maritsa shivered. 'They had *me* up there, pinned to the wall. I saw my knickers and my shoes, but my face was all shadowy... They put that stuff in my coffee and I felt sick. Then Paul came.' She found she was giggling but it didn't feel funny. 'That fat Wilhelm with his sweets and his stinky cigar...'

'And that woman,' said Sylvie, 'with her awful pong. And the others...' She went suddenly quiet.

'They were evil,' said Maritsa.

Sylvie looked at her. '*Maman* says they were devils from hell, but *we* really know, don't we?'

And Maritsa nodded.

'I hate men!' said Sylvie passionately. 'I don't ever want a boyfriend.'

'Not all men are like that,' said Maritsa. 'I'm sure my dad wasn't like that and my stepdad isn't. And I've got two horrible stepbrothers but they wouldn't really *hurt* anyone, not on purpose. They just like showing off. And what about your Marcel?'

'He's just a baby,' said Sylvie. 'Babies don't count. If he turned out like that – I'd kill him.'

'No, you wouldn't,' said Maritsa. 'He's your brother, he's your *family*.' She paused. 'There are OK cops, too...'

Sylvie blinked. 'Even OK gypsies, I suppose,' she agreed

reluctantly and for a moment she had all her old haughtiness back. 'You can be a proper friend if you like,' she offered.

'We've *got* to be friends,' said Maritsa, 'because of what happened...'

The nurse began signalling frantically.

Maritsa pulled a face. 'She wants me to go.'

'Come back,' said Sylvie. 'Later.'

'Can't,' said Maritsa. 'They're taking me home today. But I will be back. There's my gran, you see...'

Down in the Rue de Sèvres, rooftops and ledges were whitening with snow.

Maritsa hugged herself inside a borrowed coat. 'I must have the Gift,' she said, wonderingly. 'I dreamed it would snow and look, it happened!'

'If you dream of the *Loterie Nationale*,' Paul told her, 'let me know!'

He opened the door of a parked car, saluting smartly: '*Mademoiselle...*' The nurses stood on the pavement and watched Maritsa get in.

The driver wore a smart buttoned blue uniform and her pale hair was fringed below a navy-blue hat. She held out her hand. 'Hello, Maritsa,' she said. 'I'm Claire. I've heard a lot about you.'

Paul got into the back. Rose was taking up most of the seat, so he was forced to huddle against the window. She made the car stink, but no one seemed to mind.

'So where do we take you, Maritsa? Where do you live?'

'Gennevilliers,' she confessed.

'Ah,' said Claire. 'That was a good guess.'

'What was?'

Claire smiled. 'You'll see...'

Rose reached forward and tugged at a bunch of Maritsa's newly brushed curls. 'You looked at those books I gave you?'

'Oh, *Grand-mère*,' said Maritsa, turning round. 'Thank you. You're so nice.'

'Nice, spice,' muttered Rose. 'Did you practise your reading?'

'A bit. I was sleepy. I watched TV.'

'Application!' said Rose fiercely.

Claire started the engine and they moved off, Maritsa waving frantically at the nurses on the pavement.

A tourist, impressed, asked, 'Who's that?'

'Oh – some celebrity,' said someone. 'City's full of them...'

Claire followed the road to the Ile St Louis. The cathedral of Notre Dame hung in a web of snow and all its niched saints wore white lace bonnets.

As they crossed the second half of the river, the lamps along the bridges came on, ivory-gold against a speckled mauve sky.

'They say they've found me a place again,' announced Rose. 'Shan't go. They can't make me.'

Paul laughed. 'What's wrong with it this time, *Grand-mère?*' 'I'm not your *grand-mère*,' objected Rose coyly. 'I'm much too young for that!'

Maritsa nudged Claire. 'What does she mean?' she whispered. 'A place?'

'Oh, there's a vacancy,' said Claire. 'Sounds nice – a Home for Impoverished Gentlewomen.'

'They wouldn't have Rose,' giggled Maritsa.

'I wouldn't have *them*,' sniffed Rose.

In the glass tubes outside the Centre Pompidou, people seemed to float, gliding up and down the long escalators like shoals of fish.

'That ugly building,' complained Claire.

'The square is good,' said Paul.

'Good for what?'

'Busking.'

Maritsa whipped round. 'Hey,' she said. 'I thought you only did that when you were after someone.'

'Did what?' asked Paul innocently.

'*You* know!' Maritsa cried.

The shop signs in the Place de la République glittered neon and sequins, their brash colours enamelling the slushy pavements.

'I dreamed I flew over here,' Maritsa boasted.

Paul was impressed. 'You had quite a dream.'

Maritsa nodded. 'You were in it too, *Grand-mère.*' She grinned. 'You were a clown.'

'I approve of clowns,' said Rose. 'They're the only people who've got things right.'

They drove under the snow-freckled monuments of the Montmartre cemetery.

'There's a nice little place for me up there,' said Rose cheerfully.

'Oh, Gran,' said Maritsa. She suddenly noticed something. 'That van,' she said. 'It's been following us.'

'You'd make a good detective,' said Claire. She gabbled something into her radio and the van suddenly swerved and sped away.

Maritsa was thrilled. 'Was it another one of *them*?' she asked. 'Will you catch them? Will there be a car chase?'

Claire laughed. 'You've been watching too many American films.'

'And not reading,' put in Rose sternly.

They crossed a loop of the river again at Clichy.

'Put me out here,' said Maritsa, after they'd passed St Joseph's church. 'I can walk home. You'll scare my lot!'

'Sorry,' said Claire. 'You're going home in style, *mademoiselle.*'

They parked on the familiar piece of wasteland. Maritsa turned and blew Rose a kiss. 'Bye, *Grand-mère,*' she said. 'I'll come back and see you...' She tried the door but it was locked.

'Open it,' she shouted. 'Let me out.'

'Not yet,' said Paul. 'Watch.'

And slowly, across the scrubby, snow-wrinkled ground they came – her people, the *kumpania* – as if they had known, as if someone had told them. They came with candles and lanterns and plastic flowers, with an accordion and a fiddle and a new little foal born in the night, the young women with babies tucked into their shawls, the bare-legged children, the mama, ample in a shawl and flowered skirts, the stepfather with his thick black moustache and even the two boys.

'But how did they know?' asked Maritsa. 'And why aren't they working?'

Claire smiled. 'It was the good guess. We thought it might be Gennevilliers, so yesterday we sent someone out to check.'

'*Cops?*' gasped Maritsa. 'But we never talk to cops.'

'Well, some of you do.' Paul smiled. 'And anyway, one of them could speak your language.'

'I speak French now,' protested Maritsa. 'Because I want to stay here.'

'And very good French too,' said Claire. 'But don't forget your own tongue.'

'You can teach me,' offered Rose, 'if you like.'

'There's that van again,' said Maritsa. 'Over there. Look.' She tried to read the letters on its side. PATÎSSERIE. Cake shop?

People began unloading something from the back and walking with it across the snow.

Claire reached across and opened the door. 'Go on,' she said. 'Go and see what they've got.'

Maritsa climbed out and went over to look. Under snow-sprinkled cellophane, a big silver platter was mounded high with candied fruits – crystallized pears from Provence, sugared apricots, frosted plums.

'For you, *mademoiselle*,' said the cake-shop lady from the Boulevard St Michel, looking down nervously at Stefan, who was already fingering the pink curly bows.

'She can't pig up all that lot by herself,' Nikolas grumbled. 'What about us? We're hungry.' And he prised out a cherry.

The mama smacked him and made him put it back. 'She can eat the lot if she wants to,' she shouted. 'Your big sister's a star!' Then she put her arms round Maritsa and started to cry. 'Our little stray filly,' she wept. 'Thank God you're safe!' She glowered accusingly at Claire and Paul. 'And no thanks to that lot.'

Claire sounded the horn and everyone jumped.

Maritsa pointed at Rose, leaning out of the back window.

'Look,' she said proudly. 'That's my gran!'

'You haven't got a gran,' said the mama.

'I have now,' said Maritsa. 'She's there.'

Paul coughed expressively and they all waited.

'The fruits are a present to Maritsa,' he said gruffly. 'From the Paris cops. With apologies and thanks.'

Not many of them knew what he was talking about, but they all clapped.

'What are apologies?' Maritsa asked him.

'Saying you're sorry,' said Paul. 'I should never have let you take that risk.'

The fiddler had had enough of trying to understand strange foreign words. It was Christmas Eve and the lost girl had come back and that was enough.

He nodded once to the accordian player, tucked his fiddle under his chin and lifted a heavy boot to stamp out a good rhythm.

Then he started to play.

ACKNOWLEDGEMENTS

I would like to thank the dedicated compilers of the *Patrin Web Journal* for indispensable information on the Roma, and for the *Patrin Glossary* which gave me further insight into Romani usage (visit it yourself at http://www.geocities.com/paris/5121/about.htm). Another excellent source was *Études Tsiganes* (set your browser to http://www.etudestsiganes.asso.fr).

Two books which I found invaluable were Jean-Pierre Liégeois's *Tsiganes*, and *Tsiganes en Roumanie* by Bernard Houliat and Antoine Schneck. Particular thanks to Françoise Giovannangeli, who had spent some time on a gypsy site in Paris and who sent me extracts from a study by Médicins du Monde, which I would never have found without her help. Lastly, many thanks to Lee Francis of Muswell Hill library for his interest and active help.

– E. R.